MW01009850

The Graveyard Shift

Also From Darynda Jones

CHARLEY DAVIDSON SERIES
First Grave on the Right
For I have Sinned: A Charley Short Story
Second Grave on the Left
Third Grave Dead Ahead
Fourth Grave Beneath my Feet
Fifth Grave Past the Light
Sixth Grave on the Edge
Seventh Grave and No Body
Eight Grave After Dark
Brighter than the Sun: A Reyes Novella
The Dirt on Ninth Grave
The Curse of Tenth Grave
Eleventh Grave in Moonlight
The Trouble with Twelfth Grave
Summoned to Thirteenth Grave
The Graveyard Shift: A Charley Novella

BETWIXT & BETWEEN
Betwixt
Bewitched

THE NEVERNEATH
A Lovely Drop
The Monster

MYSTERY

SUNSHINE VICRAM SERIES
A Bad Day for Sunshine

YOUNG ADULT

DARKLIGHT SERIES
Death and the Girl Next Door
Death, Doom, and Detention
Death and the Girl He Loves

The Graveyard Shift

A Charley Davidson Novella

By Darynda Jones

1001 DARK NIGHTS
PRESS

The Graveyard Shift
A Charley Davidson Novella
By Darynda Jones

1001 Dark Nights

Copyright 2020 Darynda Jones
ISBN: 978-1-951812-07-2

Foreword: Copyright 2014 M. J. Rose

Published by 1001 Dark Nights Press, an imprint of Evil Eye Concepts, Incorporated

Acknowledgments from the Author

The fact that I was able to delve into the Charley universe again was beyond thrilling. I couldn't wait to get to know more about these characters. Of course, now that I do, I want even more. Such is the life.

But these types of endeavors are rarely done alone. I must thank the following people from the bottom of my bottomless, greedy-for-story heart.

First, I must thank my incredible agent, Alexandra Machinist, without whom the Charley world would not exist to such a spectacular degree. She is, simply put, a kingmaker. And my editors at St. Martin's Press, Jennifer Enderlin and Alexandra Sehulster, for loving Charley and the gang as much as I do.

I absolutely have to thank the gorgeous trio at 1001 Dark Nights, Liz, MJ, and Jillian, for being as excited to work with me as I was to work with them. What a dream come true!

And thank you so very much to the lovely Chelle Olson for making this book the best that it could be.

Thank you to my wonderful, amazing assistants, Netters, Dana, and Trayce. A.k.a., the Dream Team.

Thank you to the lurves of my life, my family, who let me hug and kiss on them in public. (Except for Netters. She fights me, but a girl's gotta do what a girl's gotta do.)

And thank you OH SO MUCH to my Grimlets! The best readers on the planet! Thank you for sticking with me, and thanks for the help with Garrett's middle name!

I hope you enjoy Garrett and Marika's story.

Sign up for the 1001 Dark Nights Newsletter
and be entered to win a Tiffany Key necklace.

There's a contest every month!

Go to www.1001DarkNights.com to subscribe.

**As a bonus, all subscribers can download
FIVE FREE exclusive books!**

One Thousand and One Dark Nights

Once upon a time, in the future…

*I was a student fascinated with stories and learning.
I studied philosophy, poetry, history, the occult, and
the art and science of love and magic. I had a vast
library at my father's home and collected thousands
of volumes of fantastic tales.*

*I learned all about ancient races and bygone
times. About myths and legends and dreams of all
people through the millennium. And the more I read
the stronger my imagination grew until I discovered
that I was able to travel into the stories... to actually
become part of them.*

*I wish I could say that I listened to my teacher
and respected my gift, as I ought to have. If I had, I
would not be telling you this tale now.
But I was foolhardy and confused, showing off
with bravery.*

*One afternoon, curious about the myth of the
Arabian Nights, I traveled back to ancient Persia to
see for myself if it was true that every day Shahryar
(Persian: شهريار, "king") married a new virgin, and then
sent yesterday's wife to be beheaded. It was written
and I had read that by the time he met Scheherazade,
the vizier's daughter, he'd killed one thousand
women.*

Something went wrong with my efforts. I arrived in the midst of the story and somehow exchanged places with Scheherazade – a phenomena that had never occurred before and that still to this day, I cannot explain.

Now I am trapped in that ancient past. I have taken on Scheherazade's life and the only way I can protect myself and stay alive is to do what she did to protect herself and stay alive.

Every night the King calls for me and listens as I spin tales. And when the evening ends and dawn breaks, I stop at a point that leaves him breathless and yearning for more. And so the King spares my life for one more day, so that he might hear the rest of my dark tale.

As soon as I finish a story... I begin a new one... like the one that you, dear reader, have before you now.

Chapter One

"Well, that escalated quickly."
—Family Motto

Charley Davidson, a god with a penchant for maiming first and asking questions later, was going to kill Garrett. No, that wasn't right. Charley's husband, Reyes Farrow, also a god with a penchant for maiming first and asking questions later, would start the whole process by ripping him to shreds, then letting Charley finish him off. Gladly. And with much glee.

Garrett had one job. One. Fucking. Job. Watch his best friends' daughter, Beep, aka Elwyn Alexandra Loehr, a kid who just happened to be destined to save the world from a catastrophic demon uprising. He was supposed to guard her with his life. To keep her safe. To protect her from all the ghosts and goblins—metaphorically speaking since he didn't have a supernatural bone in his body—hell-bent on doing her harm before she could prevent said catastrophic demon uprising.

He failed.

Yesterday, at exactly 3:33 p.m., the precocious five-year-old was running across a sun-drenched field of sagebrush and wild grasses when she disappeared right before his eyes. One second she was tripping over, well, absolutely nothing—so much like her mother, it startled him—and the next, she was gone.

If he hadn't been looking right at her, if his gaze hadn't been laser-locked on the long, dark tangles cascading down her back, if she hadn't disappeared between his strategically placed blinks, he would've questioned the entire event. But there was simply no doubt about it. She'd vanished into thin air.

The way she disappeared would suggest a supernatural influence, especially considering the fact that she was the daughter of two gods, but her celestial parents had placed a shield over the entire area. No supernatural entity could penetrate it. Was there some loophole they'd missed? Some escape clause they'd overlooked?

Garrett didn't hesitate. He immediately called in his entire team, but even his most preternaturally enhanced members couldn't figure out what had happened, and one of them was a bona fide angel. Well, former angel.

After thirty-six hours of scouring every inch of Santa Fe and the surrounding area for even a sign of the little hellion, a storm had rolled in, and the search had to be abandoned. Garrett left his team at the compound, as well as the Loehrs, Elwyn's grandparents, panicked and scrambling to figure out what'd happened. In the meantime, he went in search of the only woman he knew who could see past the veil of not only space, but time as well.

He had one clue to go on. Elwyn's last words before she took off across the rugged New Mexican terrain.

Surely, he'd heard her wrong. He prayed he'd heard her wrong as he fought the winds and icy pelts of the desert storm, then raised a fist and pounded on the door of his ex, Marika Dubois.

* * * *

Marika struggled to pull a sage green robe over her shoulders as she hurried to the door. Partly because someone was pounding on it at 3:00 a.m. Never a good sign. But mostly because whoever was pounding on it was doing so rather loudly, and she didn't relish the thought of trying to get her rambunctious son back to sleep if the noise woke him. The thunderstorm had been bad enough. Now, this.

Whatever reason made some asshole bang on her door at this hour had better be a good one, or so help her…

She swung the door open and stopped short, stunned to find Garrett Swopes on the other side—the very man she'd just this week crossed off her Christmas card list. For good this time.

She felt faint as he towered over her. Damn him. Rain dripped down his face and accommodatingly molded a wet T-shirt to the hills and valleys of his muscles, accentuating each and every one.

It took some effort, but she finally tore her gaze off the imprints his abs made in the black material and forced her eyes back to his face, knowing what she would find there. Hardness. Revulsion. Hatred.

The scowl he wore would suggest he had yet to forgive her.

The scowl she wore would suggest she didn't care.

"You're late," she said, refusing him entry despite the drenching effects of the rain.

How dare he be annoyed? She was the one who'd been startled awake by his knocking—correction, incessant pounding—at three in the morning. If anyone should be testy, it was certainly not the jackass standing before her.

Not that he was there to see her. He was never there to see her. But three in the morning? Really?

"Zaire is asleep," she added, infusing her voice with as much coldness as she could muster on such short notice. "And you were supposed to pick him up last night."

Surprise registered in his silvery eyes. The hard lines of his dark face softened for just a second before he recovered.

"You forgot?" she screeched, appalled. Then she remembered her sleeping son not thirty feet away, the door to his room slightly ajar, and forced herself to calm. Welding her teeth together, she glared right back at him. "You're a real class act, Swopes. Forgetting your own son. Come back when you're sober."

He had to be drunk. Or at least well on his way. He would never visit the likes of Marika Dubois in the middle of the night otherwise. He detested her, after all, for several reasons.

First, she'd stalked him. There was really no other word for it. She'd needed a certain type of man from a certain type of bloodline, and he just happened to be that type.

Second, she'd tricked him into getting her pregnant.

And third, she didn't tell him about said pregnancy. He found out when he ran into her and Zaire a mere month after she'd given birth. Being the seasoned actress that she was, the shock she felt rocket through her at their unexpected meeting danced in glorious Technicolor across her face.

Garrett knew. He knew Zaire was his son, and that she had no intention of ever telling him.

She had her reasons. She was trying to spare him a lifetime of guilt for being an absentee father, for one. But he didn't want to hear it. He'd never trusted her after that. Probably never would. Yet he'd insisted on paying child support and being in Zaire's life. A fact that surprised her to this day.

Still, now was not the time to go into it. She pushed the door to close it in his infuriatingly perfect face, but he easily stopped her with a hand on a panel and, God help her, she was almost glad he did. The more he stood there, the more she got to drink in the hills and valleys of his biceps. The expanse of his chest and width of his shoulders. The hard line of his jaw and full curves of his mouth.

She chided her hormones, well, the few she had left as she was quickly approaching the big three-oh, and she'd heard it was all downhill from there.

It clearly took a lot for Garrett to even stand there. His eyes glistened with animosity. He could hardly stomach the sight of her. Could hardly stand being in her presence. Not for the last few years anyway. He made no bones about it.

So, when he bit down and wrenched out the words he probably hated saying as much as she hated hearing—because who didn't enjoy seething derision on occasion?—it shocked her to the very depth of her being.

"I need help," he said from between clenched teeth.

"I couldn't agree more, but I don't know any good psychiatrists. Now, if you don't mind…"

She started to slam the door shut despite the fact that their son was asleep in the next room, but he jammed a booted foot between it and the frame to stop her. She looked through the slit, her face the picture of astonishment at his gall.

"I need *your* help," he said, his sheepish demeanor so unlike him. He lowered his head, his strong jaw working a double, as he said, "She's gone."

"What do you—?" His meaning hit Marika before she finished the sentence. Dread flooded every cell in her body.

She swung the door wide and waved him inside. After closing it, she hurried to the bathroom, grabbed a towel, and handed it to him.

"What do you mean she's gone?" she asked before sinking onto the divan.

He wiped the rain off his face then draped the towel around his neck. "She disappeared."

"What do you mean she disappeared?" She tried to keep the panic out of her voice. She failed. Apart from her son, Elwyn Alexandra Loehr was the only thing she loved on this Earth. Besides her grandmother. And the man soaking her carpet, but he would never know that.

"Please, sit down."

He indicated his clothes with a shrug. "I'm wet."

She'd noticed. A lot. "That sofa has seen worse."

"Like?"

"Like your son. Sit."

He sank down and scrubbed a hand over his face. "I mean, she disappeared. Literally. She was there one second and gone the next."

Scooting to the edge of her seat, she clasped her hands in front of her to keep from fidgeting, her most hated nervous habit. "Start from the beginning. I need to know everything."

Chapter Two

*If each day is a gift,
can I return last Monday?*
—Meme

Garrett filled his lungs and sat back. He would love to know everything. Where, exactly, his best friends were. How he'd fought his way into special forces only to end up a bounty hunter-turned-bodyguard and head of security for a single, solitary being. And how that single, solitary being, a five-going-on-thirty-eight-year-old, could vanish so completely. So absolutely. All the while, leaving no trace of where she went.

He rubbed a hand over his face then started. "We were out walking on that path just past the compound. The one behind the main house."

"The one that leads to the hot springs?" Marika asked.

He nodded and gave his ex, if one could call her that, a once-over for probably the tenth time since she opened the door. Her short, green robe—as far as short, green robes went—did little to hide her assets. The fact that they were damn nice assets had nothing to do with his admonishing thoughts. He couldn't help but wonder why she'd considered it a good wardrobe choice for answering a door in the middle of the night. But who knew? Maybe she had late-night visitors often.

Acid flooded his stomach at the thought. He swallowed hard and continued. "Yes. The path to the springs. She was running ahead of me when her bracelet slipped off her wrist."

"Oh, no." Marika knew what that bracelet meant to Beep. Hardly a surprise. The pope would've known what that bracelet meant to her if he'd taken her calls.

"I found it a few minutes later. No need to worry."

Her face, framed by soft, dark blond curls and graced with a wide mouth and dimples even when she wasn't smiling—a trait he found fascinating—relaxed.

"I slipped it back on and tightened it around her wrist."

Her tiny wrist. So thin and fragile, he worried he'd break it every time he had to put that damned bracelet back on. But he couldn't worry about that now.

He slid his brows together in thought, trying to piece together everything he'd spent the last thirty-six hours tearing apart second-by-second.

"And then?" Marika coaxed.

"Then she looked at me and said she wished I could find Osh as easily as I had the bracelet he'd made for her."

She drew her clasped hands to her chest, ever the romantic. "She loves that bracelet so much."

"She does. That and her damnable doll. Too much. I've never seen a child so…I don't know, obsessed?" She always carried around her Osh doll. She'd seen it in a shop when she was barely three and swore it was him. Osh'ekiel. A male rag doll with black yarn for hair and a top hat. It resembled the only picture she had of him. The only one they could find.

He regretted ever telling the little imp stories of Osh. She constantly wanted to hear more and more, like a child dreaming of King Arthur, a mythical hero from days gone by.

"She loves him," Marika said so matter-of-factly, he shot her a curious glare. "Is it so hard to believe a girl could love someone she's never met?" When he continued to stare, she added, "People do it all the time." She cleared her throat and dusted off an invisible piece of lint. "You know, with celebrities and sports figures. People like that."

He'd give her that. Garrett's gaze traveled to the pyramid-shaped opening where her robe parted at her legs. She had fantastic legs. But the first thing that had grabbed his attention when he met Marika Dubois was her accent. As clichéd as it sounded, he'd heard her voice from behind him in a pub. Warm and husky and tinted with a faint helping of French.

When he turned and saw her, all blond curls and thick lashes, he almost tripped. And he hadn't even been walking.

But that was her plan. She knew how to get his attention. Knew exactly how to play him, as it turned out. She flashed him a cursory smile, laid a tip on the table she'd been sharing with another man, and got up to leave.

The man had grabbed her wrist. Jerked her closer. Asked where she was going. When she reminded him that she had somewhere to be, he told her—no, *ordered* her—to sit back down until he dismissed her.

Garrett's ire skyrocketed so fast he saw stars. Just like she knew it would. The scene was played to orchestral perfection. Each line delivered with just the right pause. Just the right inflection. The man's expression full of menace. Hers full of fear, yet her chin lifted in defiance.

Garrett had been played like a heated game of Monopoly. Turned out the guy was an actor. And gay. Hardly interested in the damsel in distress.

And then there was Marika. All warmth and gratitude afterward. Garrett had, naturally, saved her from the mustache-twirling villain. Hopefully, the black eye and swollen lip made the actor rethink his choice of jobs in the future.

Of course, Garrett hadn't known any of that until months later when he saw Marika and a baby at an outdoor market, all sunshine and smiles. Well, all smiles until her gaze met his. She hadn't smiled at him since.

"Haven't you ever loved someone from afar?" she asked him.

"No."

"Are you lying only to me, or to yourself as well?"

Irritation slid up his spine. "And just what is that supposed to mean?"

She released a frustrated sigh. "Nothing. Elwyn wished you could find Osh as easily as her bracelet."

"Yes." He relaxed his shoulders, still wondering what the hell she'd meant. If anyone was in love with someone else... Then again, Marika didn't do love. Not monogamous love, anyway. She had too many men in her life to stoop to something so basic. "Osh." He thought back again. "She wished I could find Osh, and then she twirled around as though looking for him."

Marika's brows slid together. "Okay. And then what?"

He lifted a shoulder. "Don't quote me on this, but I think she said she'd find him."

"Find who?"

He shrugged again. "Osh, I assume."

"What?"

"I know how it sounds. But I swear, we were talking about Osh, and she wished I could find him. I wished I could too, but we've searched everywhere, and we just don't know where he is. Then she looked at me with those huge copper eyes, her expression thoughtful, and said, 'That's okay. I'll find him.' Next thing I knew, she was handing me her Osh doll and running off down the trail."

"Where she disappeared," Marika said.

"Where she disappeared."

"Good heavens."

"Actually, more likely bad hell. I don't think a demon would be allowed in heaven, even a slave demon."

Marika's eyes rounded. "She wouldn't... I mean, she can't. Can she dematerialize like her parents could? Can she actually, you know, go to hell?"

"That's just it." Garrett sat up and put his elbows on his knees. "We don't think she can. Once she found out her mom and dad could, she tried over and over. She has a lot of abilities thanks to her lineage, but she was never able to dematerialize. Then again, Charley didn't learn that little trick until she was in her late twenties. It could be latent."

Marika scooted closer to him. "Do you mean Elwyn could have dematerialized?"

He shook his head. "I really don't think so."

"But you don't know for certain?"

"No, I do. It wasn't like that. When Charley did it, it was instantaneous. She was just suddenly not there."

"You just said that's what happened!" Marika stood and paced, her agitation shining through.

"I know, but the more I think about it...this was gradual."

Marika frowned in thought then sank back onto the divan. "Gradual. Okay. Wait, why were you watching her? I thought you had the graveyard shift since she rarely sleeps."

"Normally, I do. But the girls' club was out of town for a bike rally."

She fought for a smile. "I bet they love being called that."

Donovan and his cohorts, the last remnants of a fairly infamous biker club called The Bandits, were also part of Elwyn's security team—which Garrett headed up. It had always surprised Marika that he took the graveyard shift until Donovan told her that Garrett hardly slept either. Said the two of them, Beep and Garrett, made the perfect nocturnal pair.

"The rain's stopped," he said, uncurling the towel from his neck and placing it on her heavy wooden coffee table. "I'm wasting time. Can you do your thing or not?"

Marika shot him a glower from beneath her lashes.

His expression changed instantly from irritation to remorse. "Sorry. But can you?"

After another quick glower, she thought about it. "I need to gather a few items. Do you have something of hers? Maybe her Osh doll?"

"It's in the truck," he said, rising to his feet. He stretched, raked a hand over his head, then shook it as though trying to stay awake.

He looked haggard, and Garrett never looked anything but magnificent with a side of dangerous, quiet confidence.

"It'll take me a little while," she said. "Why don't you go back to the compound and get some sleep? I'll call you—"

"I'm fine." His tone convinced her not to argue. Men. "I'll get the doll."

"Thank you. I'm going to"—she looked down at her robe—"slip into something a little more comfortable."

He raised a brow. Marika rolled her eyes and hurried to her bedroom.

Five minutes later she was in the kitchen, draped in a white gauze tunic and leggings, gathering a couple of things for the journey as she liked to call them. Her grandmother had taught her everything, but she had yet to take a journey without her. The woman's death still pained her, like a raw wound that refused to heal, even though it had been almost a year.

She took a beer out of the fridge and handed it to Garrett before saying, "Don't come in."

"Wait," he said, taking the beer. "Where are you going?"

"Into my bedroom. I can concentrate better without anyone watching."

He nodded. "Fair enough." He handed her the doll.

It always brought a smile to her face. Black yarn for hair. Huge, round eyes. A long, black coat and top hat. Marika realized it was probably supposed to appeal to the vamp crowd. "It's like a goth Raggedy Andy."

He laughed softly as though barely able to exert the effort before sitting on the sofa and taking a long draught of beer.

She didn't even drink beer. She only kept it in the fridge in case he showed up. How pathetic was that? He almost always picked up Zaire from her mother's house in El Dorado, a village south of Santa Fe, even though it took an extra thirty minutes to make the round trip. Anything to avoid seeing her.

He sank back and let his eyes drift shut as she gathered her supplies.

"She drinks coffee," he mumbled, the threat of sleep tumbling his thoughts. "Did you know that?"

"Elwyn?" she asked.

"Mm-hmm. And her favorite writer is Stephen King."

"You let her drink coffee and read Stephen King?"

"You say that like we have a choice. That kid is more stubborn than her mother was."

She walked over to him, and he opened his eyes enough to see her arms full of tins and vials. "Does she at least take cream and sugar?"

Lowering his lids again, he grinned and simply shook his head. "She drinks it as black as my soul. Her words. It's the only thing that calms her down. And her favorite book is *The Stand*. Has been since she was three."

"I'm not sure what kind of influence you'll be on our son."

"We tried hiding them from her."

"The books?"

"Mm-hmm. She always found them."

A minute smile played about one corner of his mouth. She'd had access to that corner at one time. Had taken full advantage of it. Wanted to take advantage again, but she supposed that would never happen. The last time they'd tried to have a relationship—for Zaire's sake—she'd thought it progressing splendidly. Then Garrett had cut it off with no explanation. It almost broke her. She swore she would never let a man rip her to shreds like that again. Especially Garrett Swopes.

"Do you know what it's like sitting in public with a five-year-old who drinks black coffee and reads Stephen King? So many glares. So, so many glares."

She sank onto the sofa beside him and laughed softly. "Thankfully, I do not."

"She only sleeps three to four hours a night."

"Coffee," she reminded him.

"You don't understand," he said, his words beginning to slur. "That's *after* the coffee. Without it, she bounces off the walls."

His broad chest rose and fell, and she knew if he stopped talking, he'd pass out. But this was the most he'd said to her in years. God help her, she didn't want it to end.

But it had to. She had to be strong for Zaire. She couldn't let Garrett know how she really felt about him, and she damned sure couldn't risk another broken heart. The last one almost killed her.

"She's up at three in the morning," he continued, "reading or drawing or doing experiments on Miss Peregrine."

She shook out of her thoughts, and asked, "Who's Miss Peregrine?"

"Her hamster."

"Oh, right. You got her a hamster for her first birthday. It can't possibly be the same one."

"It is."

"That was over four years ago. Hamsters only live two years. Maybe three."

He lifted a heavy-lidded gaze to her and shrugged. "That's what I mean. I think she keeps bringing her back to life or something. She keeps healing her."

"Wow. Like mother, like daughter?"

"Exactly."

"Well, what kind of experiments does she do?"

"She's trying to figure out the weight of its soul," he said, his lids drifting shut again. "She's decided souls have mass and therefore must have weight. And don't even get me started on the hellhounds. What she puts them through. Or so I'm told. And poor Artemis."

"The departed Rottweiler?"

He didn't answer. Instead, his breaths grew deep and even, and the beer he cradled in his hands leaned precariously to the left.

She studied them. His hands. Too rugged to be elegant, his long fingers were lean and strong, his nails clean and well-trimmed. She knew what those fingers were capable of. Had felt the metal of the rings he wore in places she recalled all too clearly when going to bed alone. Two of the rings were skulls, and he fidgeted with them when he got nervous—a habit she found oddly endearing.

"What an incredible child," she said, snapping out of her thoughts as she lifted the bottle slowly from his grasp. She put it on the coffee table before heading to her room. Or, more importantly, her closet.

Once there, she fought a dizzy spell. They'd been happening more and more often, but she had bigger things to worry about at the moment. She arranged the items around the altar like her grandmother, a powerful mambo—a priestess—had taught her. It had been so long since she'd performed the ritual of sight, she didn't know if she could pull it off. And, in all honesty, she'd only seen past the veil a couple of times. But it was in her blood. And in Zaire's blood, even more so.

Marika was the descendant of Sefu Zaire, a very powerful Haitian houngan—a Vodou priest. And Garrett was descended from an equally powerful Voodoo queen. Probably the most famous in history, Marie Laveau. It was why Marika had sought him out. Why she seduced him.

When she was a child, her grandmother, her mother, and three of her aunts had performed a ritual of sight on her, one outlawed in their religion for centuries. They saw things that changed them. Her aunt Vanessa never practiced again. Her aunt Naomi took her own life a year later. And her favorite aunt, Lovely, left and never returned. All because of what they saw that night. Yet it had very little to do with Marika herself.

They'd only performed the ritual because her grandmother, the amazing mambo Phara Dubois, had told everyone Marika was special. Gifted with sight. Destined for greater things. But who didn't want to believe that about their children and children's children?

Their vision, once they invited the loa Papa Legba, the guardian of the crossroads, to inhabit them, was more about a family living in an enchanted land with a daughter who could reap the souls of the dead.

That daughter turned out to be Charley Davidson. And Charley would have a daughter as well, a god in her own right, who would stand against Lucifer in the coming wars. Who would battle him for every soul on Earth.

They were also shown Marika's son and the fact that he would stand with the deity. Would be a part of the great battle.

It was then, as a child, Marika had decided to make her son the strongest she possibly could. She believed that by combining her bloodline with that of an heir from another great priest or priestess, their son would be just as powerful as their ancestors, if not more so. Thus, he would stand a better chance of survival. Because if her grandmother's visions were to be believed, the battle would be a bloodbath. It would rage for seven days and seven nights. And thousands upon thousands would die.

Her grandmother had never kept anything from her—until that day. She simply told Marika there was more but that she couldn't explain further. Not yet. And she never got around to giving her granddaughter the whole story before she passed.

While Marika wanted to know more than anything, she didn't dare invite the loa Papa Legba inside her just to get the rest of the story. Not after what'd happened to her aunts and, in Marika's opinion, her mother.

But tonight, she would have to invite him. While she could see deep into the veil, only Papa Legba could see through time. And she may need that.

Unfortunately, she didn't have a live chicken on hand. Zaire's goldfish would have to do. Hopefully, he wouldn't notice before she could replace it.

Chapter Three

Bacon: Duct tape for food
—Universal Truth

Garrett stilled. He felt someone close, and since he wasn't currently seeing anyone, someone hovering nearby while he slept was a little disconcerting. He kept his breathing deep and even until he oriented himself to his surroundings. And figured out how much he'd had to drink the night before.

A second later, he realized he was sitting up. Kind of. He was leaning against a chair back or a sofa. Of course. Marika's. But why was he—?

He shot up, his eyes wide as he scanned his surroundings. A soft pre-dawn light streaked across the pale curtains. He'd been asleep for hours, and Elwyn was still out there.

He cursed under his breath and grabbed his phone to check for messages. Two of his team members had checked in: Donovan, the biker pack leader and a former bank robber; and Robert, better known as *Uncle Bob*, Charley's uncle and, bizarrely, a former angel.

Garrett had the strangest life.

It grew even stranger when he sensed someone close. Right beside him, in fact.

He turned to see his son sitting beside him, his hair, curly and dark blond, a wild mop of chaos atop his head. He wore Spider-Man pajamas and sat eating bacon and playing a game on his mother's phone.

Garrett relaxed and leaned closer to him. "What are you playing?"

"Flash Code Academy," he said without looking up.

"Sounds cool." Garrett glanced up to see Marika in the kitchen, and the smell of bacon hit him so hard, he worried he'd visibly drool.

Her skin shone a pale gold, and her hands shook. He couldn't help but wonder what it cost her to see into the veil.

The phone buzzed and whistled as Zaire played, completely ignoring his father, but this was the game. Garrett leaned even closer, and Zaire stiffened. Trying not to smile, Garrett bent his head for a better look at the phone, but the kid was onto him.

"You think you got what it takes?" Zaire asked Garrett.

"To steal that bacon off your plate?"

"Yep."

"I do, actually."

"Bring it, old man."

That was too much. Garrett growled, scooped the kid into his arms and gave him a huge bear hug.

"You know," he said, after pretending to eat him alive and causing a fit of giggles, "you're awful mouthy for a five-year-old."

"I'm sorry!" Zaire shouted through the laughter.

"Do you give up?"

"Never!" He twisted in his father's arms and tried to put Garrett in a headlock.

It didn't work, but he gave the kid points for effort. Right before he took him to the floor and pinned him there so he could gnaw on his ribs.

"Do you give up?" Garrett asked again, giving Zaire yet another chance to survive his inevitable demise.

"Yes!" he finally shouted.

Garrett let him up a microsecond before his son turned the tables on him with a sassy, "Psych," and attacked, though his method of combat was more of a hug than an actual form of defense. They'd have to work on that.

In the meantime, Garrett took full advantage, pulling the boy against his chest. Zaire let him, then said, "You're still not getting my bacon."

"Here," Marika said, putting a plate of eggs and bacon with a cup of fresh coffee on an end table. "Now you have your very own and can stop torturing our child."

Our child. The words sobered him instantly. He gave Zaire another quick hug then set him back to look at him. Besides the blond curls that would someday be the envy of every girl he ever met, he had smooth, sand-colored skin and deep silvery-gray eyes—much like Garrett's, only brighter. He was the most beautiful thing Garrett had ever seen. And more than he ever deserved.

"You were supposed to be here last night," Zaire said, going back to the bacon and the phone.

"Sorry about that."

"It's okay. Mom told me." He glanced over at him, trying not to look worried. "You'll find her, right? That's what you do?"

"That's what I do."

They ate mostly in silence while Marika threw dishes in the sink and hurried to get dressed. Her movements, though graceful as ever, were harried. She was in that damned green robe again, the one short enough to double as a cheerleading outfit. She unpinned her wet hair as she rushed to her bedroom, and it fell in a sea of glistening tangles down her back. Garrett was annoyed that he even noticed.

"I know, right?" Zaire said beside him.

"What?"

"Mom. She's pretty. Everyone says so. Tommy Velasquez's older brother is in love with her. He has pictures of her on his wall."

Garrett straightened. "He has what?"

"And he's going to ask her if she'll wait for him. He wants to marry her but he's still too young."

"How young is he?" Garrett asked, appalled.

"Fourteen."

What the fuck? He gaped at his son and said aloud, "What the fuck?"

Marika popped her head out the door. "Garrett!"

"Sorry." He cringed. "Forget I said that."

Zaire lifted a disinterested shoulder, but Garrett saw the barest hint of a grin at the corner of his mouth. A mouth so like his mother's, it caused an ache in Garrett's heart. He'd wanted this once upon a time. A family. A home. A reason to breathe. But that was a long time ago, and he'd learned all too well what other men—and children, apparently— thought of Marika Dubois.

"You ready, munchkin?" she asked, trying to slide a jacket on and grab Zaire's backpack at the same time.

"I guess. But why can't I go with you?"

She chided him with a single glance. "I've already told you. Now get your shoes on."

"I need clothes."

"They're in here." She tossed his backpack to him. "You need a bath, dirty boy."

"Really?" He brightened then looked at Garrett. "Grandma's bath is like a swimming pool."

"No splashing," she warned.

Zaire fought with his shoe then waited for Marika to go grab her purse before leaning into his dad with the most wicked grin Garrett had ever seen, and whispering, "Grandma lets me splash."

* * * *

"What gives?" Garrett asked after she got back into his truck. The sun was hovering just above the horizon at that point. The brilliant colors cast a soft light on his face and reflected in his eyes. The effect enchanted her for a moment, but she sobered when his brows slid together, and he looked down to start his truck—a big black thing that rumbled when he brought it to life.

She looked back at the door to her mother's house. "Nothing. She was already up. She can keep him all day, no problem."

"I mean you," he said, putting the truck into gear and heading out.

They drove past Pueblo-style adobe houses accented with bright turquoise or dark red or sunshine yellow. Even the stores in Santa Fe were either adobe or territorial, built with indigenous materials, thick hand-plastered walls, carved wooden doors, exposed natural wood vigas, and earthy hues. It was truly the City Different.

"What gives?" he asked again, interrupting her thoughts. "You're pale and kind of greenish-yellow."

She gasped and pulled down his sunshade to look in the mirror. She was indeed greenish-yellow. "I guess the rituals take a lot out of me."

"Did you...how do you put it? Did you *see* anything?"

"Not exactly."

His shoulders fell, but just barely. "Then where are we going?"

"To the last place you saw her."

"So, when you say *not exactly*, you mean—?"

"Not exactly," she repeated.

"Marika, we are talking about the life of a five-year-old girl here."

"No, Garrett, we aren't."

He pulled to a stop at a red light. "What does that mean?"

"It means we are talking about the life of a five-year-old *god*. Yes, she's a child in her human form, but she is the daughter of two bona fide gods, Garrett. Two celestial beings. Don't doubt for a minute she can't do things you've never dreamed possible."

When the light turned green, he pulled into a gas station and put the truck in park. "What aren't you saying?"

Dread twisted her stomach into knots. What if she was wrong? What if she'd looked in the wrong place or invited the wrong spirit? "I just... I don't know."

"You don't know, or you don't want to say?"

She dropped her gaze. "A little of both."

"Marika, I'm not a patient man."

"Yes. I've noticed." And yet, he was anything *but* impatient with Zaire.

"Just tell me what you know."

"It's just...if I'm wrong..."

"Marika," he said softly as though he understood what she was going through. Then again, he probably did. He, a mere mortal, working and fighting alongside gods and angels and demons. The thought, when one allowed oneself to really contemplate it, was mindboggling.

And now she was involved, too. The fate of the human race depended on a five-year-old who took her coffee black and read horror in her spare time. And Garrett Fontenot Swopes had come to Marika for help.

She clasped her hands together to keep them from shaking. "She's gone."

He eyed her suspiciously then asked, "What do you mean?"

"I mean, she's gone. She's not on this plane."

He didn't speak for a long time as though grappling with what she'd said. He looked out the windshield, his large hands tight around the steering wheel, the knuckles on his long fingers turning white, and asked, "How is that possible?"

"This is your world, Garrett. I just live in it."

He closed his eyes, his jaw working for several moments before he spoke again. "Is she...was she taken to a hell dimension?"

"Like Charley was?" Adrenaline flooded every cell in Marika's body with the mere thought.

Elwyn's mother had been sent to a hell dimension when she defied orders from on high. On Earth, her sentence had lasted ten days. But in the dimension she'd been banished to, it lasted over one hundred years. Apparently, every dimension, every plane of existence, had its own definition of time, and they rarely aligned with Earth's.

He nodded.

"I don't know. I don't want to comment on something I have no understanding of."

He settled a knowing gaze on her. "*Now* you're in my world. I may live in it, but I hardly understand it."

"I don't envy that."

"How sure are you?"

"Very. I would never envy such a thing."

"No, I mean—?"

"That she's not on this plane?"

He pressed his mouth together and gave the briefest nod of acknowledgment.

"Eighty-five percent? Maybe eighty-six. Her aura is impossible to miss."

"What do you mean?"

"Her aura. Her energy. You know, that incredible mosaic of color that encapsulates her?"

He only shook his head.

"Wait, you can't see it?"

"No." He turned away from her. "I can see the departed as a faint, gray mist sometimes, in certain light under just the right conditions, but that's about it."

She tried to hide the look of astonishment on her face. When he turned back to her, she realized that she'd failed.

"What?" he asked.

"I just thought...you work for Charley and Reyes. You protect their daughter. Yet you can't see the departed clearly? Or auras? Or demons, for that matter?"

When he only blinked at her as if she'd grown another head, she busied herself with smoothing her jacket over her jeans.

"You mean to tell me," he started, his voice razor-sharp, "that you've been able to see the departed all this time?"

"Of course, I can see the departed. The question is, why can't you? I mean, you worked with Charley for, what? Almost three years?"

"Four. And in my defense, I didn't know what she was for the first two and a half. No, wait, three."

"Then why on planet Earth would they put you in charge of Elwyn's safety?"

"That's not offensive at all," he ground out before pulling back onto the road.

"I'm sorry. I don't mean to offend you. It's just—"

"Oh, no. I get it. I'm useless. I have no powers. I can't even see dead guys walking around at all hours of the day and night. I'm not even certain when the hellhounds are around."

"What?" she asked, her tone more a shriek than she'd intended. "You've never seen a hellhound?"

"Really?"

"You've… I just… I don't even know what to think." She put a hand over her mouth in bewilderment. "I mean, all this time, I just thought you had the sight."

"Well, I don't. Can we move past this?"

"Then why—?" She shut up before she stuck her foot in her mouth any further.

Too late. "Then why am I in charge of the girl destined to save the world? Why did they entrust me with their most prized possession? I have no fucking idea, if you must know. I'm apparently on a list of some kind that our lovely Miss Davidson had in her head." He tapped his temple to demonstrate. "Of course, no one knows who else is on this mysterious list because *Charles* didn't bother to text it to anyone before she turned herself into the Astrodome over Santa Fe."

"*Charles.* I never did understand your nickname for Charley. And, by the way, it's missus," she said softly.

"What?"

"You said Miss Davidson. It's Mrs."

"Seriously? You're correcting me?"

"Which makes me wonder, why didn't she take Mr. Farrow's last name?"

"Can we get back to the issue at hand?"

"The fact that you're completely underqualified for your job?"

He drew in a deep breath, took the next turn so sharply that Marika slid into her door despite the seatbelt, and said, "No. Beep."

She grinned.

"What now?" he growled, taking another turn, this one onto the road to the compound.

She tucked the grin away, but explained, "You called her Beep. I haven't heard you do that in a long time."

"Right. She decided when she was three-and-a-half that she was too grown-up for such a childish name."

"At three?"

"And a half," he corrected, holding up an index finger. "She got very into that. We couldn't even call Osh by his shortened name anymore. It was suddenly Osh'ekiel or nothing."

"I never met him."

"Neither had she. Not that she remembers anyway."

"That's right." According to what Marika had learned, Osh'ekiel disappeared the day of the great battle. The same day Charley and Reyes ascended. "How did she get so, I don't know—?"

"Obsessed?" he offered.

"Yes. I mean, the bracelet. The Osh doll—which is adorable, by the way." She glanced down at her purse to take another look at it.

"That would be my fault."

"Figures."

He cast her a sideways glance. "I told her about her parents. About Charley growing up. At least, what I knew. About Reyes."

"Did you tell her about you-know-what?" When he only raised a brow, she added, "About Reyes being the son of Satan. The very being she is destined to battle for all humanity?"

"Oh. No. She already knew."

Marika let out a soft gasp. "Who told her?"

"If I had to guess, one of her plethora of dead friends."

"She has departed friends?"

"Many. May I continue?"

"Yes. Please."

"As I was saying, her mind is like a sponge."

He wound up a road that would take them to Los Alamos if they stayed on it. The scenery was breathtaking. Vast and stark and beautiful, much like the man in the driver's seat.

"She can't get enough. I could talk for hours, and she'd always want more."

Marika could hardly blame her. What child didn't want to know where they came from? Who their biological parents were? What was in store for them? Especially when the storyteller was Garrett Swopes.

"Did you tell her?"

Garrett glanced over at as his riding companion. All things considered, she was taking everything really well. Then again, she knew much more about his world than most.

He thought back to all the talks and the bedtime stories he'd told Beep. Her grandparents told her stories, too, though they didn't know near the extent of all things Charley Davidson and Reyes Farrow. But Garrett wondered just what Marika had told her. She kept Beep every once in a while. Playdates with Zaire. But knowing the child as well as he did, surely she bombarded Marika with question after question.

"Did you tell her about Osh?" she asked him.

"Yes and no. She found a box."

"A box?"

"The container we'd stored his things in. She'd always been curious about him. The Loehrs told her who'd made her the bracelet she'd worn since she was a baby, but they only knew he was supernatural in some way."

He was supernatural in the most supernatural way possible.

Five years ago, Osh'ekiel—his Daeva name that Beep insisted they use—had disappeared the same day as her parents. Since Garrett had no supernatural abilities himself, no way to help in a fight against a demon army, they'd sent him away that day with instructions that should anything happen to them, he was in charge. He was to watch over their daughter.

The rest of the group, the supernaturally endowed members anyway, battled an army of otherworldly demons dead set on taking over this dimension. They'd almost succeeded, too, but Charley'd had a plan, and damned if she didn't pull it off.

Garrett had never been more impressed with the impish Charles Davidson than he had been that day. But it'd ended as quickly as it began, and then they were gone. Just...gone. They'd ascended and scattered their collective energies over Santa Fe, a mystical city in its own right, to form a shield, a protective barrier to keep their daughter safe.

Their only lapse in judgment had been leaving Garrett in charge of Beep's safety. If Osh were still around, slave demon from hell or not, Garrett was certain the girl would be at home, wreaking her usual havoc.

Still, so much of that day didn't make sense. Charles had sent Osh to watch over Beep during the battle five years ago. To keep her safe, which, in hindsight, Garrett had always thought odd. One of their most formidable allies, a powerful entity who fought his way out of hell, sent to babysit?

To this day, it made no sense to Garrett, especially after he found out that Osh had never made it to Elwyn's side that day. He'd disappeared. Apparently, there was a lot of that going around.

Of course, Elwyn was more than just the daughter of two gods. It had been prophesied that she'd challenge Satan in a great battle. If she won, mankind would once again be safe for at least a thousand years. If she lost, hell would be unleashed upon the Earth.

Garrett had been to hell once. He did not care to repeat the experience here on Earth. And if Elwyn Alexandra Loehr wasn't found before Satan decided to storm the gates and unleash his legions upon the unsuspecting multitudes of humans, that was exactly what would happen. According to prophecy. One that Garrett himself had uncovered. Some days, he wished he could cover it back up.

Chapter Four

What (and I can't stress this enough) the fuck?
—T-shirt

Garrett pulled into the compound, the area mostly empty of the workers and security teams that usually populated it. Only Beep's grandparents were home at the moment. They lived in the main house.

"I've called everyone back, but it'll take a while."

"For?" Marika asked.

"We need to regroup, especially with this new info. Robert may know something. What could have taken Beep off the plane?"

"Right, the former angel."

Garrett bit down. "And to think, we've been arguing for weeks."

"We who?" she asked, her slender brows sliding together.

"All of us. The Guard."

"The security team? About what?"

"About what to do with her. Elwyn. Some want her in kindergarten next year, and some want her in high school. We've gone back and forth, delved into every pro and con, and we still can't decide. Of course, it's ultimately up to the Loehrs, but they don't know what to do either."

The Loehrs were Beep's grandparents, Reyes's biological parents, who'd been entrusted to raise mankind's most precious—if not frustratingly precocious—gift.

"She needs both," Marika said matter-of-factly as she raised her phone in the air, searching for a signal. *Good luck with that.*

"Well, yes. That's what I said. But it's impossible."

Marika almost had a bar of service. Her face fell when it disappeared. "Not at all."

He turned off the engine and rested an elbow on the steering wheel. "I'm listening."

"She needs the socialization of children her age," she said, giving up and putting her phone into her bag. "At the same time, she needs the intellectual stimulation she can only find in a secondary education setting. Or even higher, quite frankly."

When Marika spoke, her mouth moved in soft, whispery waves. Much like when they kissed, but that had been a long time ago.

"And what do you propose?"

She blinked at him. "Both. Aren't you listening?"

Garrett tried not to grin. "How do you propose we give her both?"

"She goes to kindergarten in the morning and high school in the afternoon."

He felt his lids narrow in thought. "They can do that?"

"Of course."

"And it wouldn't be weird?"

"Maybe, but we are talking about the daughter of two gods. Who's to say what's weird and what isn't?"

"True." He let out a long, frustrated sigh. "Do you know how long we've been arguing about this?"

"Do I want to know?"

"No. Let's go."

The compound, with its main house and multiple outbuildings, was originally a monastery. They'd spent eight months in an abandoned convent on the other side of the mountain while Charley was pregnant. Sacred ground and all. A monastery was nothing new, but it did seem to impress Marika whenever she made the trek to pick up Zaire.

She hopped down from the truck, stopped, and drew in a deep breath. "I love this place. It's so serene and beautiful."

Garrett looked around. Every building had been remodeled before they moved in. A project that would have taken years only took a couple of months when one could afford a small army working day and night.

One thing Reyes and Charley did not skimp on leaving their daughter was money. She was an heiress in every sense of the word. But that was one story Garrett had yet to tell her. He prayed he'd still be able to one day.

"Okay," Marika said, sobering. "We're basically under a canopy. A supernatural shield, right?"

He cupped a hand across his brows to block the low morning sun and nodded.

"And we're on sacred ground."

"One more level of protection."

"And the compound is full of your security team, surrounded by hellhounds, and backed up by a departed Rottweiler who served as guardian to Charley and now Elwyn."

"All of the above. Any supernatural entity that wants to do Beep harm will be blocked. In theory anyway."

"Then if something did take her, if something meant to do her harm, how did it get past all of that?"

He tilted his head. "That is why you're here."

"Right." She slung her bag over her shoulder. "Show me exactly where she disappeared."

"This way." He pointed and led the way around the main house to the wilderness trail behind it.

Marika started forward, hesitated, then followed him, all the while scanning the area with a wary expression on her face.

"What?" he asked as they made their way up the trail.

"The hellhounds."

He stopped and turned to her. "You can see them?"

"Of course." She turned her head, her gaze stopping periodically on this spot or that. "And what a sight they are. Nothing that could see them, supernatural or not, would choose to go up against the likes of twelve massive beasts."

"Even Buttercup?" When she pinned him with a questioning gaze, he explained. "Beep named them. All twelve. And one is named Buttercup."

Marika snorted softly. "Right. I knew she named them. I can't tell them apart, though, so I've never bothered to learn their names. My question is, does the hellhound know he's named after a princess in a modern fairy tale?"

Garrett grinned even though the thought of that day, the one where the little minx had christened all twelve hellhounds with a glow-in-the-dark fairy wand, caused the chasm in his chest to open up and swallow him whole. "What if we can't find her?" he asked.

A hand slid gently up the biceps on his right arm. "We will," Marika said, her tone determined. "We have to." When his gaze traveled from the small hand on his arm back to her face, she pointed and asked, "Is that the spot?"

He shook out of his temporary trance and focused in the direction her index finger indicated. "Yes. Exactly. How did you know?"

"Don't you see it?"

Alarm prickled across his skin. He stepped closer. "See what?"

"A departed." She started toward it, but he took her arm and went ahead of her.

"Friend or foe?"

"I don't know." She curled her fingers into a death grip on his shirt as she followed. "He doesn't seem completely coherent."

"In what way?"

"He knows we're here. He's very aware of our presence, but he's staring past us. He's tall, Caucasian, with a ragged blue coat and a knit cap. And he seems angry."

"Damn it. I need Robert. We have several…regulars, but hell if I know what they look like."

"I'll try to talk to him, but I have to tell you, they rarely acknowledge my existence."

"Really?" Garrett asked, glancing down at her from over his shoulder. "Even if you can see them?"

"Yes. I think it's because I'm not really part of the club." She eased past him toward the spot where Beep had disappeared.

"First, what does that mean? Second," he said, taking hold of her arm, "can he hurt you?"

"I was born sensitive to the spirit realm. My grandmother felt it the moment I entered the world. But I had to learn to see them. If I travel beyond the veil, I can see them easily, but I had to learn to see them in this world. The physical one. I sometimes wonder if they don't talk to me because I am somewhat of an outsider to them. An interloper."

"You can explain that later. And second?"

"No, he can't hurt me. At least, I don't think so." She stopped, nodded to the departed, and forced a smile onto her face. "I'm Marika, and this is Garrett." She gestured toward him.

"What's he doing?" Garrett asked.

"Staring." She turned to look behind them and then shook her head. "I just don't know what he's staring at. There's nothing there that I can see." She refocused on the departed. Either that or she was as good an actress as he'd suspected her of being on occasion. "It's like he's in a trance. Catatonic."

"Could he have taken Elwyn?" Garrett asked, his voice sharper than he'd planned. Frustration was ripping a hole in his stomach.

"I honestly have no idea." Her gaze drifted up to his, her hazel eyes glistening in the morning sun, her expression pained. "I'm sorry. He's not giving me anything."

Garrett fought the urge to smooth the worry lines from her face. "Don't be, Marika. Ask him about Beep. Elwyn. Call her Elwyn."

With a nod, she cleared her throat and tried again. "Can you please help us? We need to find Elwyn. Elwyn Loehr."

She gasped and looked back at Garrett. "He shook his head. Just barely."

"Try again," he said, adrenaline racing through his veins.

Stepping closer, she asked, "Do you know where she is?"

After a moment, she winced and put a hand over Garrett's. The one he had hold of her with. The one he was squeezing around her slender arm too tightly.

He eased his hold but didn't let go completely. "Sorry. I just...we don't know what happened. He could be anything but a simple departed. You haven't seen what some of these guys are capable of."

"It's okay. Thank you."

A part of Marika sang in joyous harmony that Garrett would care enough to hold onto her. Well, they would have if her insides could sing. He stood so close that she could feel the warmth of him. His strength. The power that lay just beneath his rock-hard surface. Either his nearness was making her dizzy, or she still hadn't fully recovered from the ritual.

There was, of course, a third option, but she wasn't going to acknowledge that one at the moment. Denial was a beautiful thing.

"What's his name?" Garrett asked. "I know several of their names."

She turned back to the departed man, his stone-like expression full of fury. But besides the one gesture, he didn't move.

"What's your name, hon?" she asked. "Are you a friend of Elwyn's?

Elwyn Loehr?"

The departed did it again. Shook his head, the movement so infinitesimal, she wondered if she'd imagined it.

She decided to test him, and said, "Elwyn?" When he didn't move, she added, "Elwyn Loehr."

Again, the barest hint of a shake.

"You didn't see her?"

He didn't move.

"Is it her name that you're shaking your head at? Elwyn Loehr?"

"Not anymore," the departed said in a harsh whisper, though he still didn't move or drop his gaze from the horizon beyond. He curled his hands into fists at his sides, and Marika took an involuntary step back.

"Did he say something?" Garrett asked.

She held up an index finger. She would explain later, but at the moment, she needed to get what she could out of this guy. "It's not her name anymore? She changed it?"

Nothing. Back to stone.

Garrett spoke softly in her ear. "You gotta give me something."

She pretended his voice, his nearness, wasn't quickening her pulse. After a perfunctory nod, she continued. "What's your name?"

No reaction.

"Did someone take her? Did you see someone take her?"

"Wait for it," the guy whispered, then his irises shifted to his left. "Wait for it."

Marika turned, but again, saw nothing. She fought a wave of dizziness, furious that her own body would betray her so malevolently, then asked him, "Wait for what?"

When she turned back, the departed was staring straight at her.

She stumbled back against Garrett, then righted herself as quickly as she could, ignoring the hand he slid over her ribs to offer extra support, the stirring warmth that soaked through to her skin. "Wait for what?" she repeated.

"You'll know." He gestured to his side with a nod.

She looked again, but when she turned back to him a second time, he'd vanished. "Damn it," she said, stepping out of Garrett's hold and turning in a full circle to search for the man.

"What?" Garrett asked, scanning the area as well.

"He disappeared."

"Him, too?"

"No. I mean, yes, but he's pure spiritual energy. He can do it at the drop of a hat. Did you see where he was gesturing?"

"You forget who you're talking to."

She grew as frustrated as Garrett, though more with herself than the situation. "No offense, but you are of absolutely no use to me."

"That's harsh," he said, taken aback. "What'd I do?"

"Nothing. That's the problem." She started to walk away, but he stepped in front of her. She stopped just short of barreling into him, filled her lungs, and said as patiently as she could, "You are blind. I need you to see, Garrett."

"See what?"

"Them."

He narrowed his eyes. "*Them* them?"

"*Them* them. Elwyn's life could depend on it. And if…*when* we get her back, you need to be able to protect her from any enemy at her gate, not just the ones you can see."

She sidestepped him. He followed.

"I get it," he said. "Trust me. But there's nothing I can do about it. And arguing is not going to suddenly make me see dead people. We need to—"

Marika whirled around to face him. "But if you could. If you could see them, would you want to?"

"I…I guess, but it's a moot point."

"So, if there were a way, you'd definitely want it? It's a big decision, Garrett. One I was going to bring up later, but—"

His gaze turned wary, the gray in his eyes shimmering like silver silk. "Why are we talking about this?"

"Because there might be a way to make it happen. Remember, I couldn't see them either. Not in the physical world. I had to learn."

"That sounds great, but we don't have time."

"We need to make the time. I need your help to find her."

"Right. I'm of no use to you as I am."

Feeling a bit sheepish, she lifted a shoulder. "Something like that."

After a long moment of contemplation, he asked, "You aren't going to spread chicken blood on me, are you?"

"No." Thrilled he was caving, she took his wrist and led him to a flat rock bench.

"Wait, we're doing this here?" he asked as he sank onto the seat. "Now?"

"No time like the present. Hold this." That morning while Garrett slept, she'd prepared the materials she'd need. She handed him a small leather pouch filled with herbs and spices.

He took it and crinkled his nose. "What's in this?"

"You don't want to know." She handed him another pouch filled with human bone fragments and white sand soaked in a sparrow's blood. "Put one in each hand."

He frowned at her but obeyed.

Garrett had always wondered what it would be like to really see the departed in all their glory. Not just the occasional gray blur. Would it freak him out? He doubted it. He'd been to hell, after all. Seen people in all manner of horror. How much worse could seeing the departed on Earth be?

"What do these do?" he asked, turning the pouches this way and that.

"Nothing. They're the distraction."

"What?" He looked back at her to find a hand cupped in front of his face. Before it registered what she was doing, she blew into her hand.

A white powder billowed out of her palm and clouded his vision. He jerked back, but the shock had caused him to gasp—which was probably the witch's plan—and he inhaled a large portion of the powder deep into his lungs.

He reared back. Blinked. Rubbed his eyes and doubled over in a fit of coughs. "What the fuck, Marika?" The world tilted to the side, and he fell to his hands and knees. She'd just dosed him with LSD.

Chapter Five

Fifty shades of cray.
—Coffee Mug

"Was that LSD?" Garrett asked, his body burning.

"Just relax."

He felt Marika's hand on his shoulder. He shook it off and tried to stumble to his feet.

"I wouldn't do that just yet."

"Fuck you. What was that? What did you—?" His tongue thickened in his mouth, and he fought to form a simple sentence. When he tried to focus on his surroundings, they melted. The trees. The sagebrush. The clumps of wild grasses. The sun dripped down from the sky and melded with the mountains, their colors mixing to create an entirely different landscape, exciting and new.

Oh, yeah. It was definitely LSD. Or something like it.

He heard Marika's voice from far away. "Garrett, you need to sit down. This part won't last long."

He felt blindly for the bench to help him balance, but he couldn't quite make it. Waves kept crashing into him, pushing him over like a rag doll. Suddenly, he wondered if he still had feet. He couldn't feel them. Could he normally feel his feet? Panicked, he searched for his hands to no avail.

"Garrett, you're hyperventilating. You need to slow your breathing."

He tried to tell Marika exactly where she could shove her pseudo-scientific advice, but his voice sounded like a cassette tape that had been eaten. *Those were the days.*

"That's better," she said, her voice soothing, but he didn't remember doing anything to make it better. Was he sitting on the bench? He couldn't feel his ass. Did he still have an ass?

Panic shot through him again. Women liked his backside. If that was gone, what else did he have to live for?

"Slower," she said, her voice like a cool ocean wave at night.

He could smell her. Her scent reminded him of the first time he'd cruised a boardwalk in California. The salt on the ocean breeze. The spun sugar in the cotton candy. The perfume of a girl who'd smiled at him, rich and warm like vanilla. The scent and the smile.

"Garrett, look at me."

He shook his head.

"Open your eyes, sweetheart."

"I can't. I don't have any." He realized she was on her knees between his legs. A very dangerous place to be.

"You do. I promise."

"Do I still have an ass?"

She chuckled softly, the sound smooth and calming like bourbon easing down his throat. "You most definitely have an ass. And eyes. Open them."

He tried to pry his lids apart. After several failed attempts, he finally succeeded. The world had taken shape again, and yet it hadn't. It was somehow different from the one he'd been in only moments earlier.

"I don't remember it," Marika said, her voice sad. "The world you just left. But I remember it was beautiful, especially New Mexico."

"What do you mean?" He turned to her and her face...she was stunning, swimming in a sea of greens and golds. The colors of her hazel eyes had been amplified a thousand times, and they flowed like water around her. Then he realized she had streaks on her face.

"Is that blood?" he asked, trying to focus.

She took out a wipe and smoothed it over her skin. "It's part of the ritual."

"So, there was chicken blood involved?"

"No."

Then he saw the cut on her wrist. "It was your blood?"

"I needed human blood. It'll heal."

He reached out and ran a thumb over her mouth. "You are absolutely beautiful. Like a mermaid."

"Uh-oh." She bit her bottom lip, and he would've sold his soul to do the same. It was just so bitable. "I forgot about this part. My grandmother warned me, but I was a kid when she did this to me. I hadn't…reached that stage yet."

"What stage?"

"The, um, coupling stage."

"Ah." When he let his hands slide down her neck, she took it into hers.

"How do you feel?"

"Wonderful." And he did. Suddenly, every molecule in his body hummed with energy. Some of them leaked out and collided with hers, crashing into her like he wanted to do.

"That's good. I need you to take a deep breath to steady yourself, then look to your right."

"That would mean looking away from you."

"Yes, it would. But only for a second."

He caved, slowly turned his head to the right, and fought two urges at once. The first was to grab Marika and run for his life. The second was to black out.

He lurched to the side and backed off the bench, falling backwards onto the ground.

Standing next to the bench was the biggest, blackest werewolf-bear-looking dog he'd ever seen. Only it wasn't a dog. Its fur was scalloped as though it had scales. They were covered in an iridescent silver powder that seemed to change color with each movement. And if Garrett didn't know better, he'd have sworn that molten lava flowed underneath its oddly textured fur. An orange glow leaked from between the scales when the creature moved.

The canine slowly advanced, its massive paws eating up the ground faster than Garrett could crab-walk away. Its quivering lips were pulled back in a snarl that revealed a mouthful of huge, razor-sharp teeth.

Marika laughed and reached out to pet it. Garrett started to scramble to his feet to save her, but he'd barely moved when he realized the dog wasn't going to attack her and feast upon her intestines.

Instead, it stopped snarling and nuzzled her neck with a soft, deep whimper.

"This," she said with a giggle, giving the massive beast a few solid pats, "could be your Buttercup. I'm not one hundred percent sure, though. I have a tough time telling them apart."

Garrett was still on his back, unconsciously putting as much distance between himself and the beast as he could.

"It's okay," Marika said, walking over to him. "He was just giving you a hard time. They're very playful."

"That's a hellhound," Garrett said, never passing up a chance to state the obvious. The hound stood head-to-head with Marika. It wasn't a dog. It was a dragon.

"It is indeed a hellhound." She reached down to him.

He cast her a quick glower, suddenly humiliated, and stood all on his very own. "Beep sketches them," he said, brushing himself off. "I just thought she sucked at drawing."

"And now?"

"Girl has real talent."

The hellhound eased closer, and Garrett took an involuntary step back. Thankfully, it wasn't interested in him. It wanted more nuzzles from Marika. He could hardly blame the beast.

"Wait. I thought we couldn't touch the departed. That they weren't solid to us."

"We can't," she said, rubbing her face against the beast's neck even though it looked like the scales would shred her skin. "This isn't a departed. If the hellhounds want to let you see them—or even touch them—they can. It's entirely up to the alpha. Except when it comes to Elwyn, of course. I assume any spiritual being is solid to her, much like they were to her mother."

Garrett nodded just as the beast turned to the horizon and lowered his head. After expelling a throaty growl that rumbled deep and low, it tore across the field, kicking up patches of dirt and gravel before it disappeared.

"Would one of the hounds have taken her?"

"I don't think so," Marika said, gathering up her supplies. "Why would they? Unless they did it to protect her. But she's not on this plane. I'm certain of it. Where would they have taken her?"

"You're asking me?" He sat back on the bench before his knees gave out and looked around. "Is she dead?" He pointed to an older

Native American woman standing just outside the tree line in the distance.

"Departed," Marika corrected. "And, yes." She took out a moist towelette, knelt down in front of him again, and began wiping his face.

"So, that's it?" he asked, taking her in. "You just blow some powder into my face, and I can suddenly see? Anyone could do it? Any person alive could breathe that shit in—which tasted like vomit, thank you very much—and be able to see dead people?"

"Of course, not." She blotted the tissue around his eyes, but he hardly felt it. His whole face felt numb. He was afraid to ask her what the white substance was. Too short-acting to be LSD. "The person must already be sensitive to that which lies beyond the veil. Their mind simply needs to be opened a little further."

"What does that mean?" he asked. "Sensitive to that which lies beyond the veil."

"It means you. Your heritage. Your experiences. Your training." When he didn't comment, she continued. "You come from a long line of people with supernatural abilities. And you have done things few on Earth have done."

He took the wipe, pressed it against his eyes, and leaned back against the bench. "Like?"

"You have been to hell, for one."

"That sucked so hard."

"I don't doubt it. You've fought demons and kept company with gods."

"Who, might I add, are not always the most hospitable hosts."

"You've also wielded a celestial knife. One that could kill any supernatural being, spirit or demon or god. Did you think none of that would rub off on you? That it wouldn't leave a mark? A trace of its power."

He lowered the wipe, leveled a grim expression on her, and asked, "This is a baby wipe, isn't it?"

"They're very handy," she said defensively, grabbing it away from him. "Especially with a five-year-old."

"Speaking of five-year-olds, this isn't getting us anywhere. What did the dead guy say to you? Wait." A strange thought hit him. A thought he'd had when he was tripping on the vomit-flavored psychedelic powder. He studied her for a long moment, her blond hair, the pert shape of her nose, the delicate lines of her jaw, then said, "You were the girl."

"I'm sorry?" She packed up her supplies, took out the Osh doll, and then looked back up at him.

"The girl on the boardwalk."

She stilled for a solid thirty seconds, then asked, "What are you talking about?"

"I remember." He nodded as he thought back. "I was...I don't know, seventeen. Maybe eighteen. And you were at the boardwalk in California."

"Don't be silly." She stood and scanned the area.

He stood, too. "No, it was you. I remember your smile. And the way you smelled. The way you always smell. Like the beach and vanilla."

Marika slammed her lids shut, her face warming with mortification. She knew her cheeks would glow a bright red if they weren't already, so she turned away from him. But she could still see him from her periphery, the astonishment evident on his handsome face.

"Yes." He pointed at her. "I remember. You sent a friend over with a note."

"I've never been to Santa Cruz."

He crossed his arms over his chest. "I never said it was in Santa Cruz."

She'd started to argue when she realized her mistake. Instead, she stuffed the Osh doll back into her bag to cover the fact that another dizzy spell had washed over her, and the world was tilting haphazardly to the left. "Yes," she admitted at last.

She watched as he tried to come to terms with what he would likely see as yet another betrayal.

He shook his head in thought, as though trying to wrap it around his latest discovery, then gaped at her with a mixture of astonishment and...what? Disgust? Repugnance? Revulsion? "That was fifteen years ago. How the fuck long did you stalk me?"

She whirled back and regretted it instantly. "I didn't *stalk* you. Well, not back then. I was simply doing research."

"Is that what they called it?"

"Do we really need to talk about this now? We need to find your ward. You remember? Our son's best friend?"

The silver in Garrett's irises flashed with a dangerous glint. He conceded, but he was not happy about it. "We will come back to this."

She raised her chin. "I expect we will."

"And we've gotten nowhere." He turned away from her in frustration and studied the spot where he'd last seen Elwyn.

He said something else, but Marika didn't quite catch it. The earth beneath her feet suddenly felt unstable. Her balance unsteady.

Garrett turned as though expecting her to answer him, but she'd missed what he said again.

Maybe it had nothing to do with her condition. Maybe the aftereffects of the ritual were still coursing through her veins. Or perhaps she'd been awakened at three in the morning after only going to bed an hour earlier. Still, the earth shook around her and then tilted on its axis. If Garrett hadn't been right there, she would've fallen, and few things were more embarrassing.

Bed hair, maybe. Or excessive flatulence.

"What's wrong?" he asked, hauling her back onto her feet then dropping his hands.

She swayed but kept her footing. "Did you feel that?" she asked, trying to shake the cobwebs from her mind.

"Feel what?"

She swayed again, and he put a hand on her elbow. She rubbed her temple then looked up at him. "It's like I'm still in the ritual from this morning and the ground was pulled out from under me. Something shifted. Papa Legba is still keeping watch, and he's trying to tell me something has changed." She didn't understand. The loa was no longer inside her, but she'd never had a spell quite this disorienting.

"Papa who?" he asked. "Never mind. Does this have anything to do with Beep?"

Still fighting to gain her bearings, Marika looked past him to where she felt a pull of energy. A shift in the fabric of space and time. She squinted. Shook her head. Blinked, then looked again. "I'm definitely still in the veil."

He leveled a worried expression on her. "What makes you say that?"

She pointed to a clearing a mile wide. "Because there is no way that thing is of this world."

He glanced over his shoulder just as a creature unlike anything she'd ever seen before spotted them and started running directly in their direction. She took in its features between terrified heartbeats. An alien being at least eight feet tall, maybe nine—or twelve, come to think of it—raced toward them, eating up the ground as fast as a racehorse.

It looked like something from a comic book. Or a horror movie. Its shoulders were massive. Its head triangular with black horns like a ram's, and rubbery spikes sprouting from between them in mohawk fashion. Though it looked like it weighed a thousand pounds and wore thick, scaly body armor, shimmering and blood-red, it moved like an Olympic sprinter. That same crimson covered the lower half of its face, a mask hiding its nose and mouth. But not its eyes. The closer it got, the more Marika could make out the emotion that seemed to radiate out of its gaze: fury.

Marika, on the other hand, couldn't move at all. She stood pinned to the spot, her fight-or-flight response refusing to come out of sleep mode.

It was all so surreal, and she thanked the supreme being, Bondye, that the creature could not cross from its plane onto hers. Because that thing could do some serious damage if it did. Especially with the giant spear it carried. A spear... She blinked again and focused on it. A weapon drenched in blood.

"Look," Garrett said, his tone wary, "I get that I'll see things I probably don't recognize, but what the fuck is that?"

Marika's jaw dropped to the ground as one other aspect of their situation sank in. She curled her fingers into Garrett's shirt. "I don't think it's dead. Or on another plane."

The creature was close now. Perhaps only fifty yards away. Mere seconds from them at the rate it was traveling.

Garrett circled a hand around her arm and started to back up. "How do you know?"

"The dead are quiet. When they walk. When they run. They certainly don't sound like a herd of elephants tearing up the ground as they race across it."

"Son of a bitch."

* * * *

Garrett's instincts were not what they used to be. He could blame the ascending sun. Claim it blurred his vision. Or, better yet, the vomit powder, which had definitely blurred his vision. But he should have been hightailing it back to the compound the second he spotted that thing. Instead, he stood there staring like an idiot as it barreled toward them.

By the time his sanity returned, it was too late. There was no way they could outrun it.

He pushed Marika so hard that she almost fell. "Run!" he shouted, keeping his gaze on the instrument of his impending death.

Then again, maybe it just wanted to talk. If not for the fact that both it and its spear were drenched in blood, Garrett could have taken solace in that thought.

"Get to the compound!"

He tore his gaze away to search for a weapon. Anything, because he doubted his pocket knife would do any good.

The beast was close enough for him to hear its heavy breathing. He took a precious moment to turn to Marika who hadn't moved an inch. He grabbed her roughly and shook.

"Go, damn it!" he said, shoving her in the direction of the compound again.

She cradled her bag to her chest, her eyes like saucers, and took off toward the closest outbuilding.

When the beast changed directions and began following her, Garrett stepped into its path.

It refocused on him, its eyes a sea of black, and showed no signs of slowing down. Garrett braced himself, readying for the impact. When it hit him, he felt as though he'd been ripped in half.

Pain exploded inside him, and he wondered if that was what it felt like to lay on a grenade. Later, he would register Marika's scream, but at the moment, all he could think about were the stars circling the darkened edges of his vision, and the fact that he was going to die. He would fail his best friends. And Beep. And Zaire. And Marika.

Marika. What would that thing do to her?

He slid across what felt like a mile of terrain, through bushes and cacti as the beast once again went after the only woman Garrett had ever truly loved. With Herculean effort, he rolled out of the slide, skidded to a halt, and bolted like a sprinter from the starting blocks.

The beast was almost on Marika when Garrett rushed him from the side. He slammed his shoulder into the beast's rib cage with every ounce of strength he had. That time, they both slid across the inhospitable terrain.

But the creature was fast. Much faster than Garrett. Before he could gain his footing, the beast had him by the throat. That was when he noticed the massive claws. Because, why not?

It lifted Garrett off the ground with ease while letting loose what he could only imagine was a battle cry.

At least in his incompetence, Garrett had accomplished one thing. He'd managed to dislodge the creature's spear. Not that it registered until he glimpsed the long, heavy weapon out of the corner of his eye. And the woman holding it.

Panic spiked so hard and so fast he saw stars again.

"Hey!" Marika shouted, and she looked like a rabbit provoking a wolf. A fierce hare, but prey nonetheless.

The second the beast looked at her, she shoved the spear with a guttural grunt toward his face and then stumbled back, tripping on her bag.

It was one in a million, the jab she landed. The bloodied tip of the spear lodged in the creature's right eye. It reared back, dropping Garrett in the process, and pulled out the weapon with a cry of pain. And anger.

Garrett dove for the spear, hoping to wrench it out of the beast's grasp. But again, it was too fast. It swung at Garrett, its claws slicing across his back, leaving a trail of fire in their wake.

He landed on his stomach, and the beast raised the spear. Garrett would be impaled in a matter of seconds, so he did the only thing he could think of. He brought out his pocket knife and stabbed it into the top of the beast's foot.

The spear sank into the ground next to him, grazing the skin over his ribs as the beast wailed once more. But Garrett wasn't finished. He pulled out the knife, circled his arms around its leg, and slid the razor-sharp blade across its Achilles. This thing may be a different species, but Garrett knew enough about anatomy to know it had to have some kind of tendon to allow it to walk upright. It was almost human in structure.

It stumbled back, crying out in agony, then took off on all fours toward the ponderosas just past the wilderness trail, dragging its injured leg behind it.

"Garrett!" Marika screamed, and he could feel her hands on his shoulders.

He tried to turn over, but his back was on fire. As were his ribs. And his head. He decided to just lay on the ground awhile. He was about to tell Marika to get in his truck and get the fuck outta Dodge when he heard a male voice. Robert Davidson, Charley's Uncle Bob.

"Swopes!"

He'd get her to safety.

Garrett looked up at Marika, at the wetness in her eyes and on her cheeks as she smoothed a hand down the side of his face. Then he said in a weak voice, "I think we should get married."

Chapter Six

But did you die?
—Motivational Poster

Garrett lifted his lids slowly. Partly because it hurt to move even that much, but mostly because he could see dead people now. He had no idea what awaited him on a daily basis from that moment on. Hardly a checkmark for the pro column.

"Think he'll live?" a male voice asked. Donovan, the leader of the pack, a.k.a. the biker club, stood to his right.

Robert, on his left, answered. "The doc says he will."

"Doctors have been known to be wrong."

"That's true." Eric, another biker, chimed in. "A doctor once told my aunt she was healthy as a horse. Would probably live forever. She died two days later."

"What from?" Robert asked.

"Hit and run."

"Is there a reason you guys are in my…where am I?" Garrett croaked.

"You're in medical," Robert said. "And yes."

Garrett suddenly remembered the attack. "Marika?" he asked with a breathy gasp.

"She's fine." Donovan gestured toward a couch nearby. Marika lay sleeping, bundled in a sea of pale blue blankets.

"I guess she told you?"

"She did." Robert's brows slid together. "I have no idea what she described, but hell if I want it traipsing about the countryside. Unfortunately, we haven't been able to find it."

"What the fuck?" Garrett asked, his voice thick with sleep and probably lots of drugs. It would be the good shit, too. The trust Charley and Reyes left for Beep's care could afford it.

The compound housed their own medical wing, as strange and bizarre accidents seemed to happen around them often. They had a doctor on call 24/7. One who had to be brought into the fold because of Beep's peculiar physiology. She looked human, but there were subtle differences that set her apart from other children. Far apart. They needed someone they could trust, and Dr. Lucia Mirabal had been an old friend of Charley's from high school. Truth be told, she hadn't seemed all that surprised when they explained the particulars of what they would need with a personal doctor and the anomalies she would find with her primary patient.

It could've been her friendship with Charley growing up, or it could have been the money. Either way, the physician was thrilled. It allowed her time to volunteer at a couple of medical centers on local reservations.

"We wounded it," Garrett said, annoyed. "It should have left a trail of blood."

Donovan nodded. "It did. And we followed it until dark."

Robert frowned in thought. "We had to call off the search. We can't try to face something like that at night."

"I understand, but we need to find it at first light."

"Garrett," Robert said, his face grim. "Do you think…?" He swallowed hard, and wetness formed between the man's lids. "Did that thing take Elwyn?"

Garrett closed his eyes and bit down. A fiery pain shot through his face and jaw, but he didn't ease up. He needed to snap out of it. "I don't know. I just don't think so. I could see it. Marika said it wasn't a supernatural entity. It was as solid as you and me. Nothing, you know, *took* Beep. She just vanished."

"You're awake," Marika said.

Garrett watched her scrap with the blankets before freeing herself and running to his side, almost knocking Donovan down in the process. Then he saw the bruise on the side of her face and wondered when that had happened.

"You're hurt."

She shook her head. "I'm okay. How are you? That thing almost ripped you in half."

"Almost? I was sure it'd succeeded."

She forced a smile and slid a hesitant hand into his.

"So," Eric said from the edge of the bed, "when are you two getting hitched?"

Garrett stilled. Well, stilled more. Then he shot a look of horror at Marika when the memory of what he'd said to her returned.

Eric chuckled, as did Michael, the third member of the now very small biker club, who stood leaning against the doorframe to the room, clearly too cool to come in and express concern like the rest of them.

Michael was the epitome of calm reserve, a trait Garrett would have loved right about now because he suddenly remembered proposing to Marika. A woman he'd sworn he would never marry.

The comment caught her off guard. She studied him, both embarrassed and shocked at the question if her expression were any indication. When he looked away, suddenly self-conscious, she cleared her throat and took back her hand.

"Don't be ridiculous," she said to Eric. "Garrett was joking. We do it all the time."

"Right." Eric pressed his mouth together and stepped away from the bed, but Garrett got the feeling he was disappointed. Oddly enough, he was fine with that. Eric could kiss his ass.

To put an end to the awkward moment, a female voice yelled from the hall. "Oh, my God!"

He grinned and watched as Robert's wife—and Charley's best friend—Cookie Kowalski-Davidson, rushed into the room, carrying two cups of coffee. She drank a lot of coffee.

She pawned both of them off on her husband and draped herself over Garrett, being careful not to actually touch him. But she did kiss his cheek. And his temple. And his forehead. Then back to his cheek.

"Damn, Robert," Michael said. "Aren't you keeping your girl satisfied?"

She straightened, her thick black hair a mess atop her pretty head as she glared at him—though Garrett doubted she was very serious.

He'd seen her serious side. He'd seen what Charley's disappearance had done to her. She fought hard to hide it, but no one could hide that kind of pain.

"You shush," she said, shaking a finger at him. "I have a bone to pick with you."

"Shit." Michael almost straightened. Then he relaxed again. "What'd I do now?"

"Two words: brand-freaking-new Harley."

"Technically, that's four." When she glowered at him, he raised his hands in surrender. "Hey, it's not my fault transportation came with the gig. Check the contract."

"There's a contract?" Eric asked, crestfallen. "You got a contract?"

The Elwyn Loehr Foundation took care of everyone on Team Beep. Charley and Reyes had set everything up as though they'd expected to leave. Some took more advantage of that fact than others, though Michael had never been one of them. He must've really needed a new bike. Garrett wouldn't fault him for that.

Marika spoke softly, and he could tell she wasn't sure where she fit in. "Maybe we should get back to the problem at hand."

They all turned to her.

"She's right," Cookie said, taking one of the cups of coffee and moving back so they formed a circle around his bed. "I've been doing some research. Which is your department." She chided him with another glare. "I just can't find anything on the creature that attacked you."

Pride swelled inside Garrett. "You consulted the books?"

The books was code for the dozens and dozens of manuscripts and letters he'd been combing through for years, searching for any mention of the demon uprising to come. Anything that could help Beep in her fight.

"Oh, goodness no," she said, appalled. "The internet. For any sightings or lore."

He almost laughed and thought better of it. "And?"

"Like I said, nothing. Well, nothing recent. There were a couple of ancient references, but I consigned those to the same level of lore as mermaids and Big Foot."

"Right. What about you?" he asked Marika, but only because she seemed lost in thought. Judging by the lines between her brows, it wasn't a good thought.

She bit her lower lip, then said, "Something changed, Garrett."

He gave her his full attention.

"Something shifted right before we saw the creature. Like in the universe. Something—"

"Opened up?" Robert asked.

She frowned at him. "Opened up?"

"It's like you told us," he explained. "That thing is not of this world."

Garrett struggled to wrap his head around Robert's meaning. "So, by *opened up*, do you mean a portal?"

Cookie breathed in a small gasp.

"Do you disagree?" Robert asked Garrett.

He shook his head, then winced with the effort. Then flinched again from the effort it took to wince. It was a vicious cycle. "I don't disagree, and it could make sense. Since I can't—correction, *couldn't*—see into the celestial realm, I suppose a portal could've opened up."

"Oh, please, no," Cookie said. Robert led her to a chair and helped her to sit down.

"We aren't certain, gorgeous," he said, calming one of the few people on Earth that Garrett had ever truly loved. Cookie was the most genuine person he'd ever met, and he would give his left kidney just to ease her concerns. "It's just a theory."

"One that fits," Garrett offered thoughtfully. "But did Marika tell you about the dead guy on the trail?"

"Departed man," she corrected. "And yes, I did."

"He was standing at the exact spot where Beep vanished."

"It could mean something," Robert said. "I just don't know what."

Cookie pressed a hand over her heart, her face the picture of agony. "A portal," she whispered.

Robert rubbed her shoulder. Cookie clearly knew what that meant.

"My only other theory has been shot to hell," Robert said.

Garrett raised a brow. "Which was?"

"That Elwyn suddenly learned to dematerialize. If that's the case, she could've rematerialized anywhere on Earth. But according to Marika, she isn't *on* Earth. She's not even on this plane. Which would support the portal theory."

"Good heavens."

"It would," Garrett said, his mind replaying Beep's disappearance over and over. "But I just don't think so."

The doctor came in, always the professional, and ignored their conversation. She changed his IV bag, then checked his vitals. "He gonna live?" Eric asked.

She grinned, a strand of her dark red hair falling from her hair clip when she nodded. "'Fraid so." She held up a tiny flashlight and checked Garrett's pupils. "I put something in your IV. I think it will help you heal a little faster."

"That's great, but how about a snow cone?"

"Oh!" Cookie said, jumping up. "We just got a shaved ice machine. You know, for those of us who get a little hotter than others."

The doctor laughed. "Unfortunately, I don't think that's what he meant."

Impressed, Garrett asked, "You knew what I meant?"

"Of course. And snow cones are illegal. No coca-laced Mary Jane here." She pulled out a syringe and held it up so he could see it. "But I have something pretty close."

He laid his head back. "Thank you, sweet baby Jesus. Wait," he said, right before she stuck it in his IV tube. "Will this knock me out?"

"When we have a nine-foot, feral creature with claws the size of Kansas running all over the world? No way. We need you up and at 'em."

He chuckled softly then moaned. "Thanks, doc."

Marika couldn't help but notice how pretty the young doctor was. She had known they had one on staff, but she had never met her. She dropped her gaze and spotted a towel they'd missed underneath his bed. It was soaked in dark blood.

Irritation spiked within her. "Shouldn't he be in a hospital?" she asked, her voice as sharp as a scalpel.

The doctor sobered, but Robert spoke before she could. "Dr. Mirabal's the best, sweetheart. She has access to things other doctors…well, don't."

"Of course." Everyone in the room seemed to trust her implicitly. Especially Eric, who couldn't take his eyes off her. "I didn't mean to suggest otherwise."

"It's okay," the woman said before offering Marika a reassuring smile. "I know how much he means to you."

That statement caught her off guard, and she felt heat rising to her cheeks.

The doctor looked back at Garrett, her expression changing to one that brooked no argument. "I need to check that back every couple of hours," she said to Garrett. "I mean it this time."

This time?

"But your ribs are healing nicely. You should be able to walk in a few—"

"Now?" Garrett asked, interrupting. "I should be able to walk now?"

She pursed her lips in admonition. "It'll be a big risk."

"It'll be a bigger one if I don't."

"Since you put it that way..." She started to leave but turned back to him. "Just so you know, I had to sedate Mrs. Loehr. Poor thing. She's beside herself with worry."

Marika recognized the look of guilt that flashed across Garrett's face. A face that should have been swollen and bruised, but was healing at an alarming rate. She wondered what the doctor had meant when she said that she'd given him something to help him heal faster. How was that even possible?

The doctor left, the bikers went to grab something to eat, and Robert led Cookie into the hall, ordering her to get to bed. He was certainly the only one who could order that woman around.

"Wait, it got dark?" Garrett looked at Robert when he walked back in.

"I'm sorry?"

"You said it got dark and you had to stop searching."

"Yes."

"Fuck. How long have I been out?"

The muscles in Robert's jaw jumped before he gave a reluctant reply. "You aren't going to like it."

"You're going to like it even less if you don't answer."

Unphased, Robert said softly, "Almost twenty hours. It'll be light again soon."

Garrett shot up and then doubled over as pain gripped him. Marika rushed to his side, feeling helpless. She didn't like feeling helpless.

She pushed at his shoulders. "You have to rest."

"Marika, whatever cocktail the doc gave me wouldn't allow me to rest even if I wanted to."

"What?" She felt her lids round. "What exactly did she give you?"

"Who knows? That woman is gifted."

"Gifted or not," Robert said, "you still need to eat before we head out."

"Head out?" Marika asked.

"I'll grab us something."

"You can't head out."

"Thanks," Garrett said, completely ignoring her.

"You're injured."

"I need a shower, too."

"You need a lobotomy. You almost died."

"Mrs. Loehr brought some of your things." Robert pointed to an overnight bag underneath the sofa Marika had been sleeping on.

She must've slept through the woman's visit. She adored Mrs. Loehr. And Mr. Loehr, for that matter.

"You got this?" Robert asked Marika.

"I've never done a lobotomy."

Garrett swung his legs over the side, his muscles tense, his breathing labored.

She released a long, drawn-out sigh. "I suppose."

"Back in five."

After Robert left, Garrett draped an arm around her shoulders, and she helped him to his feet. "This is such a bad idea."

"So was yellow dye number five, yet here we are. Sit me back on the bed for a minute."

She did, almost dropping him in the process. He grabbed the rail with a shaking hand and then stabbed her with a glare. A glare! After everything she'd done.

"What?" she asked, exhausted and fed up with his attitude.

"Why did you risk your life for me? I told you to run."

He was angry with her? Now? She planted her fists on her hips, only now realizing that her clothes were a mess. "You may be the head of this security team, but I don't work for you. Remember?"

He leaned closer to her. "I told you to fucking run."

"And the day you're authorized to tell me what to do, I'll listen. Are you going to shower or not? I need to message my mother."

"Why didn't you run?"

"You needed my help."

"Bullshit."

"Apparently, you hit your head harder than I thought. I saved your life, if you'll recall."

"And risked yours in the process." He scrubbed a hand down his face. "Zaire needs you."

"No," she said, trying not to let the sudden rush of sadness infuse her voice. "You're stronger than I am. He needs to learn how to fight. How to survive. My mother can teach him the magics he'll need. But only *you* can teach him to fight."

"Ah, so you have it all figured out."

She reached an arm around his waist again, encouraging him to stand. "I've had a lot of time to think about it."

"What do you mean?"

"Garrett, what do you think drives my every heartbeat? My every waking moment? Our son." She conveniently left out the part about Garrett himself. Some things were better left unsaid. "He is all that matters. Him and Elwyn and Osh'ekiel. Zaire will have a much better chance of survival if you…are in his life. If you raise him."

He narrowed his eyes. "You act like you're not going to be around."

"I'm just saying. If something were to happen to me…"

"Like what?"

"Fine." She stepped away from him. "I'll shower first. I have no idea what's in my hair, but it's horribly unpleasant."

"There's nothing wrong with your hair." He raised a hand and brushed his fingers softly along her cheek and jaw. "When did that happen, exactly?"

"I don't remember." She pushed his hand away. "And why do you do that?"

"Do what?"

"One minute, you're ice-cold. And the next, you're blisteringly hot and practically hitting on me. It's not fair." She reached around him again to hoist him up, being careful of his back, which she had yet to see. "I'm putting a moratorium on flirting. And," she added with a warming scowl, "marriage proposals."

"I'm never ice-cold."

"Please. I have the frostbite to prove it."

He rose to his feet again amid several grunts and groans. "I'm sorry."

"No, you aren't. Are you good here?" They'd hobbled into a walk-in shower, complete with safety bars and a non-slip floor.

"No. I need help with my bandages."

"Oh, right." She untied the gown and slid it off him.

Ignoring his flirtations was one thing, but ignoring his ass was quite another. He had an athlete's ass. The kind that caught girls off guard as he strolled by. She should know. Her gaze slid to the bandages, covered in streaks of dried blood. "Are you sure it's okay to shower?"

"The doc would've said something if not."

"Right." *The doc.* Jealousy was so beneath her. And yet…

One giant piece of gauze covered his entire back. Marika peeled the tape around the edges slowly to the sound of his hisses and sharp intakes of breath. Served him right.

At one particularly sensitive area, he reached back and wrapped a large hand around her hip. Then he squeezed. She didn't know if it helped him or not, but it certainly helped her. He'd done that so often when they were together, his strong hands on her hips. Her thighs. Her breasts. The sensation flooded her body with memories. Unwanted ones.

Even if he did learn to care for her again, it would do either of them any good. She didn't have enough time. Unless she ended up in the twelve percent success rate. Twelve percent. The odds were certainly not in her favor.

She slowly peeled the gauze away from his back. Some of it stuck and had to be plied with the gentlest pressure she could manage, but he seemed to be doing better with each passing second. She, however, was not.

The bandage fell away, and so did the floor from beneath her feet.

Chapter Seven

Courage is knowing it might hurt and doing it anyway.
Stupidity is the same, and that's why life is hard.
—Meme

"Hold on there!" Robert's voice drifted toward Marika from far away.

He rushed into the bathroom, and he and the now-naked Garrett Swopes steadied her. Somehow, she'd ended up molded against Garrett's front side. Like his torso. And other things. Other gorgeously formed things.

"Fucking hell, Swopes," Robert said. He'd seen his back as well. "I might just pass out, too."

"Really?" Garrett grinned. "How bad is it? I feel like I'm due a few battle scars."

"You damned sure got them."

"How can you laugh?" Marika asked, unable to stop the inane welling of tears between her lashes.

"Hey." Garrett lifted her chin until she stood gazing up into that silvery gray that had become her favorite color in the world. "I'm alive, right? We're both alive. And next time I meet that thing, I'll be better prepared."

She nodded but couldn't get any words past the lump in her throat.

"I would kiss you, but there's an ex-angel in the shower with us."

"Right. Sorry," Robert said. He looked at Marika. "You weren't kidding about those claws."

She hadn't been. Garrett had four jagged lacerations spanning the distance between his upper right shoulder and left hip, but they were far enough apart to cover the majority of his powerful back. Some areas were wider than others, the flesh left open like ripped paper.

"No stitches?" she said at last.

"The doc said they really aren't deep enough to worry about it," Robert said. "Because the wounds are so jagged, she'd have to go in and cut perfectly good flesh away in order to stitch them up."

"And with the cocktails she's created," Garrett added, trying to see his back in the mirror yet not letting her go, "these will heal in no time."

"How is that possible?" she asked.

He looked down and winked at her. "We have a secret weapon."

He pulled her closer, and damned if she didn't let him. So much for her moratorium.

"Anyway," Robert said, interrupting, "I brought you both something to eat, and Cookie found some fresh clothes, too. If you want to change, Marika. Get dressed quickly, though. We head out in twenty."

"You know," Garrett said after Robert left, "we could shower at the same time."

She stepped out of his arms. "You aren't taking my wishes seriously at all."

"Sure, I am." He turned the shower on. "What wishes would those be?"

But she had moved on. They were heading out in twenty minutes. Going after that thing. Fear clawed at her throat and tore at her resolve.

"Garrett," she said, lost in the image of the creature coming at them.

"Hmm?"

She fought the urge to watch the water cascade over his immaculate shoulders. "There is something I've been wondering since we first saw the creature."

Garrett looked down at her, at her fragile exterior, so pale and ethereal, and realized he really, really, really wanted her in the shower with him. That cocktail the doc had cooked up was working wonders.

"What the bloody hell did it eat for breakfast to get that size?" he teased, but her worried expression sobered him.

She put a hand on his arm despite the water and said, "Where did all the blood come from?"

Garrett fought the wave of dread the image evoked. He'd wondered that exact same thing.

He washed like the place was on fire so Marika would have a chance at the shower. Little minx closed the door, blocking his view. What the hell? She was in and out almost as quickly as he'd been, and when she opened the door, the scent that hit him almost dropped him to his knees.

She stood there, wrapped in a towel, drying her hair. That familiar vanilla and beach scent washed over him. As if it radiated out of her. He quickly pulled on his jeans to help hide the evidence of what the woman did to him. Even he had to wonder at his ridiculous behavior. It'd been almost five years since he caught her in the arms of another man. And dolt that he was, he'd gone to her house to propose. He'd sworn right then and there that he'd never sample that particular piece of succulent fruit again.

She looked through the clothes Robert had brought. "How do you know so much about their world when you've never fully experienced it?"

"Research. I've been scouring ancient texts for years. And I'm getting pretty good at reading Latin. Just don't ask me to pronounce anything."

She stood and gazed at him with, dared he say, a look of adoration. But she sobered quickly, as though he'd caught her with her hand in the cookie jar, and looked away to rifle through the clothes again.

"It takes me months to get through the simplest text, so don't think too highly of me."

"Oh, I would never."

He caught her biting her lower lip before she gave up and took the entire bag into the bathroom.

"I'm just going to take my sandwich with me. They're leaving in five. I'll call you as soon as I know more."

The door burst open and slammed against the opposite wall. "What?" She stood in her bra and panties, a jaw-dropping set with a mix of pink polka-dotted satin and black lace.

He hesitated a solid minute then held the sandwich out to her, a turkey with green chile and swiss on a hoagie bun that'd had his mouth watering before she showed up. Now, his mouth watered for an entirely different reason. "Did you want this one?"

"You are not leaving without me."

"What?" He frowned at her, genuinely confused.

"Don't even think about it."

"You're joking, right?"

"I most certainly am not." She jerked a loose T-shirt over her head so hard, he heard it rip. She didn't seem to care. She picked up the jeans Robert had brought and hopped into them.

He watched with voyeuristic fascination as they slid over her slim hips and shapely ass, before snapping back to attention. "Marika, you're not going back out there."

She straightened in a huff, her eyes flashing like laser beams. "You brought me into this game at the bottom of the ninth. You are not benching me now."

"Sports metaphors? I figured those were beneath you."

"And I figured dumpster diving was beneath you, but it's the only way to explain your wardrobe."

He chuckled, still not entirely convinced of her dedication to the cause. His wardrobe was excellent. "No, really. You can't go. You're not going. No fucking way, no fucking how."

Ten minutes later, they were eating their sandwiches in the back of Robert's SUV. She'd tricked him. It was the vomit powder. It had to be. She could now control him with her mind.

"What's the plan?" he asked, ignoring his sandwich. The same one he'd drooled over earlier. Instead, he checked his weapon for the third time before holstering it then checking the safety on his assault rifle.

"Wait," Marika said. "Slow down."

They were headed across the rugged terrain near Diablo Canyon. Donovan sat in the passenger's side, and Garrett and Marika sat in the back.

She rewrapped her sandwich and rolled down her window. "Do you hear that?"

Robert nodded. "Howling. Is it the creature?"

Eric and Michael were behind them on their bikes. As soon as they got close, their motors drowned out the sound. Apparently. Garrett had never heard anything in the first place.

She jumped out of the still-moving vehicle, and Robert slammed on the brakes. Garrett watched as she ran to the guys on the motorcycles and gestured for them to cut their engines. Robert did the same with the SUV.

They stepped out and listened. Nothing at first, then…

"How the hell did you hear that?"

"Is it the creature?" Robert repeated.

"I don't think so. It sounds like—" She spun around to Donovan. "It sounds like Artemis."

Donovan had been Artemis's original owner before the Rottweiler died and became Charley's guardian. Then Beep's.

Donovan looked around, even though he couldn't have seen her if she were right in front of him. Out of the bikers, only Eric could see the departed, thanks to an unfortunate demon possession some years back.

Before Garrett could get a bearing on the howl that bounced off the trees and rocks surrounding them, Marika took off at a dead sprint.

"Shit," he said, gathering up his weapons and following her. "Marika, wait!"

But she was gone. Disappeared into the tree line. "Follow us on the bikes!" Garrett shouted as he took off after her. Little sprite was quick.

"Marika, damn it," he said, knowing she couldn't hear him. Though, to her credit, she did seem to be on the right track.

"Artemis!" he heard her yell, but he couldn't figure out why she was so worried. The dog had passed years ago. It wasn't like anything could hurt her. Could it?

He finally caught up to Marika when she tripped on a tree branch. She righted herself quickly and headed deeper into the forest.

They were on reservation land now, and it was land Garrett didn't know well.

"Marika, wait," he said through huffed, labored breaths.

While the cocktail the doc had given him worked wonders, it seemed to be wearing off. Pain clutched at his sides, and his back was on fire.

When he finally caught up to Marika, she was kneeling in the dirt, trying to coax Artemis to her. And after knowing about the dog for the past six years, Garrett finally got to see her.

She was a beauty. Black and tan in all the right places. Enough muscle to make her look buff. But her face was angelic. Dark, expressive eyes.

While Marika attempted to coax her closer, Artemis seemed to be trying to get Marika to follow.

"So, that's her," he said, kneeling beside the escape artist.

"Isn't she gorgeous?"

Another howl split the air around them, and Garrett almost tripped trying to leap to his feet. Though the cry wasn't from Artemis, she joined in, adding her own.

"Is that wolves?" Marika asked.

"Maybe. I mean, it has to be, right?"

Robert ran up to them then, followed quickly by Donovan.

"Is she okay?" Donovan asked.

Marika knelt down again. "She appears to be. But something is wrong."

"Elwyn," Robert said, rushing past them to follow the dog.

"Beep?" Garrett asked, taking off as well, but not before he grabbed Marika's hand.

They heard the bikes shut off in the distance. They could only take the Harleys so far in this terrain. It was too bad they weren't a dirt bike gang. Those would've come in much handier.

They ran through the forest, branches scratching their faces, but Robert was a man on a mission. "There's only one person alive Artemis would watch over like this," he said over his shoulder.

He was right. Artemis, along with twelve hellhounds and a veritable army of both the living and the dead, lived only to protect Beep. Could she really be out here? If so, how? She hadn't been on this plane—

Robert skidded to a halt. Garrett did the same, and Marika slid into his back a microsecond before she took a sharp intake of breath. Deep, guttural growls bounced off the trees around them. Blood-soaked trees. Broken trees, some of them ripped completely in half.

Both Garrett and Robert raised their rifles. Donovan raised a pistol when he showed up, and Marika kept a death grip on Garrett's shirt.

In unison, as though the movement were choreographed, they all dropped their gazes to the shadowed ground around them.

Marika's hands flew to cover her mouth as they took in the carnage they now stood right in the middle of. Half a dozen hellhounds lay wounded. Some of them looked dead. Others panted, their tongues hanging out, their gazes blank.

"What's going on?" Donovan asked, unable to see the hounds. But he did see the battlefield on which they'd fought. He saw the blood.

Artemis whined and Army-crawled closer to one of the wounded hellhounds. It whimpered back at her, and she lay a few inches from it.

"What the fuck?" Garrett said in a harsh whisper. "What the hell happened, Robert?"

"The creature." He started to kneel by one of the hounds when a low growl sent static electricity coursing over his skin.

They turned in unison to see a girl no older than thirteen or fourteen surrounded by the remaining six very healthy hellhounds. Her head was down. Her spear, much like the creature's, at the ready, both hands gripping it as though she were prepared to charge.

Garrett lowered his weapon and motioned for the other two to do the same. Correction, four. Eric and Michael had entered the arena and had their weapons trained on the girl as well.

"We won't hurt you," Garrett said, confused as ever because the girl looked entirely human. Yet, like the creature, she carried a spear and was covered almost head to toe in blood. For some reason, he hoped it wasn't hers.

She didn't move a muscle. Just watched them from beneath hooded lids partially obstructed by thick locks of long, ink-like hair that looked as if it hadn't been brushed in weeks.

Garrett raised a hand in surrender and knelt to put his semiautomatic on the ground. "We just want to know what happened. Did the creature do this?"

He stood again, minus the rifle.

She didn't move, but he could see her gaze flit from one intruder to the next as though sizing up her opponents. Then, with painstaking slowness, she sidestepped to one of the hellhounds, keeping her spear trained on the group.

Garrett's heart seized when she knelt down and poked the hound with the spear.

The hellhound whimpered, but Garrett quickly realized she wasn't hurting him. She was assessing him. She spared the briefest of glances at the wound, then refocused on the group, raised a bloodied wrist to her mouth, and tore at it with her teeth.

Marika tightened her fingers on his shirt as they watched the girl drip her blood into the hound's wound and then its mouth.

The hound shook its head, immediately coming out of its stupor, then struggled up onto all fours.

"Robert, what's going on?" Garrett whispered.

Uncle Bob didn't answer. His brows were drawn in concern, but he didn't waste a single breath with a haphazard guess.

Just then, Garrett remembered that the hellhounds could let humans see them if they wanted to. He cast a quick glance over his shoulder and realized the rest of the group could definitely see the enormous beasts. A classic combination of shock and awe reflected on each and every face around him.

"She's healing them," Marika whispered at his side as the girl moved to the next hound.

Even though her wound was fresh, she had to bite her wrist again to get the blood flowing once more. It was so savage, Garrett felt for the girl. Marveled at her bravery.

He didn't hold out much hope for the hound, though. It was one of two that Garrett had taken for dead. It didn't move even when she dripped her blood into its mouth, again without shifting her gaze from the group. When it still didn't move, she risked a quick glance, bent over and put her mouth near its ear.

It sprang to life, exactly like the first one had, shaking its head as though trying to regain its senses.

"This is magnificent," Donovan whispered, clearly impressed.

Garrett agreed.

The girl repeated the trick until only one hellhound remained sprawled on the forest floor. The one Artemis kept watch over.

She whimpered when the girl got near and pawed at the dirt. The hellhound had been gutted. The fact that it was still alive was a bit of a miracle.

This one seemed to concern the girl more than the others. She wiped at her cheek, smearing blood across her face, and Garrett realized she was crying. She whispered something to the hound and cradled its head with one arm, keeping the spear in the other. All the while, she cast nervous glances at them.

Finally, she lowered the spear and leaned it on the hound for easy access should she need it. Then, to everyone's seeming surprise, she bent over and started to scoop up the hound's intestines.

It released a sharp cry, but she continued until she had most of the innards back inside the hound's body cavity. Then she raised her bloodied hand and once again tore her wrist open with her teeth. This time, however, she went deeper, dousing the wound with her blood and then letting it flow into the hound's mouth.

The hellhound licked his jowls, but it did him no good. He didn't recover like the others. He lay on his side for several minutes, his breaths slowing until he stopped moving altogether.

The girl's chin quivered as she bent over him. The group forgotten at last, she buried her face in his neck, but only for a second. She drew in a deep breath and ripped at her wrist again. The act wrenched a sob out of Marika as they watched the girl fight for the hound's life.

She forced its massive jaws apart, pulled its head toward her, and let her blood drip into its throat. Then she ran her hand down the outside of it as though trying to force it to swallow.

Artemis whimpered again, and the other hounds, the giant, bearlike lot of them, circled their fallen comrade.

The girl had power. No doubt about that. But bringing a celestial creature back from the brink of death was not one of them. Or so Garrett thought.

As they looked on, the hound's side began to rise and fall. The group grew even quieter if that were possible, listening for signs of life. Suddenly, it shook its head, emitted a guttural groan, and scrambled to its feet.

It was like watching a newborn colt trying to gain its footing. It fell and then picked itself back up again, only to stand on wobbly legs.

The other hounds were ecstatic. They jumped and growled and nipped at each other playfully. Even Artemis got caught up in the revelry, wagging her tiny nub of a tail and barking at the playmates who were several times her size. It was like comparing her to a Chihuahua, only in reverse. Even the birds started singing, all of them joining in on the festivities. All except the girl.

When Garrett looked up, she was gone. He whirled around, just in time to see the tiny thing, spear clasped in both hands, rushing toward him so fast he could hardly make her out.

Time ceased to exist as he watched her. She was going for his heart. It was her best option. And she would have met her mark if Marika hadn't jumped in front of him. He watched as the tip of the spear, which had been only inches from his chest a heartbeat earlier, pierce Marika's throat. It was like a slow-motion scene in a movie.

Disbelief warred with instinct, but before he could react, Robert shouted, his voice hard enough to slice through the air with razor-sharp precision. "Elwyn!" he said, and Garrett leveled a stunned expression on the tiny girl.

Chapter Eight

If your path demands that you walk through hell,
walk as though you own the place.
—Meme

Every person there stood so still they could've been mistaken for statues from a distance. The three bikers all had their pistols aimed at the girl's head. Garrett didn't dare move because Marika's backside was molded to his front. If he moved, she moved. She'd stepped in front of him. She'd risked her life to spare his, and it was all for nothing because he was going to kill her.

Marika froze with the tip of the spear at her throat. If she even swallowed, it would sink deeper.

But the girl was the stillest of them all. Powerful and wild and in complete control. She hovered the spear unflinchingly at Marika's throat but kept her gaze on Garrett.

"Elwyn," Robert said again, softer this time. "Look at me, pumpkin."

Her delicate brows drew together, and Garrett could see several scars on her face. One reached from her temple down across her lips, ending at her chin. The wound had been deep, and that realization disturbed him most of all.

Robert stepped forward, but the girl—Elwyn—didn't tense. She didn't move at all. She didn't even look at him. It took Garrett a few seconds to realize that her eyes were welling up again. He couldn't believe he hadn't seen it before. Those shimmering copper irises, so unusual, so distinct. And yet, he'd missed it. And the bracelet on her wrist. The gold one that Osh had given her before he disappeared. It shimmered in the sun streaming through the branches, plain as day.

A droplet of wetness slid over her lashes, and her breath hitched in her chest. Without another thought, she dropped the spear and ran into Robert's arms.

The rest looked on, their faces the picture of astonishment as Robert swallowed her in a hug. He swayed with her, his shoulders shaking with sobs.

"Oh, my God. Where have you been? Where have you been?"

Her slim shoulders shook as well, but she didn't answer. Garrett didn't even know if she could.

After a long moment in which the hellhounds, now healed and sensing no danger to their ward, disappeared one by one, Robert set her at arm's-length. He looked her over. Pushed her hair back to examine her face. Lifted her wrist to study the damage she'd done by repeatedly biting into it.

"Are you hurt?" he asked, his voice thick with emotion.

She shook her head, and he pulled her into another hug. A soft, light laugh escaped her.

It was then that Garrett realized that Marika was in his arms. She rested her head against his shoulder, her face alit with joy as they looked on.

"Do you remember everyone?" Robert asked at last, finally releasing Elwyn.

She kept her arms locked around one of his, almost hiding behind him before turning toward the rest of the group. She glanced from one man to the next, then to Marika. Giving up her need for safety, the girl stepped closer to Marika and lifted her fingers to where she'd pierced her skin. "Brave."

Marika sobbed into a hand and, unable to contain her emotions any longer, pulled the girl into a hug. Garrett wanted to join them but held back. Beep hadn't suggested that she'd recognized him yet.

When she finally looked up at him from behind the hug, her tiny frame even smaller than Marika's, almost as if she'd suffered through years of malnutrition, she said, "Did you two finally get married?"

Garrett thought his heart would explode. He wrapped them both in his arms, one of Beep's sliding around his waist.

"Holy fuck, kid. You scared us to death."

"I'm sorry."

He hugged her harder, then asked, "Did you think that we hurt the hellhounds?"

She looked up at him. "No. I knew it was Hayal. I can smell him everywhere." Her speech was a little stilted, a bit hesitant, but she still spoke almost perfect English. Yet she spoke it with an accent, almost like Scottish with a bit of Greek mixed in. "I thought you'd come to take them. As *guouran*. As a trophy."

Just then, she looked past him at Donovan, who was still in shock if his unhinged jaw were any indication. Elwyn gave Marika one last squeeze and then headed to him.

"You remember me, yes?" she asked.

He laughed and shook his head. "You got taller."

"Maybe you got shorter," she countered, then she lifted her hand and ran her fingers along the curve of his mouth and over his scruff.

"She used to do that," Garrett said softly to Marika. "She always ran her hands over his face. Something about the scruff."

"You have scruff."

"Yeah, but he's a master at it. He's the scruff master."

"I can hear you," Donovan said.

"Well, I don't blame her," Marika said, crossing her arms over her chest. "I'd run my hands over his face too if it weren't awkward and unsettling."

Garrett started to laugh, then scowled down at her. "How long have you had that urge?"

"About twenty seconds."

Beep moved on to Eric, the youngest of the bikers. She beamed at him. "Prince Eric."

He laughed and pulled her into a tight hug. "Your mother used to call me that. She said I looked like a prince."

Elwyn giggled and stood back. "Silly rabbit. That's not why she called you that."

Before he could ask her what she meant, she moved on to Michael.

Ever the placid bad boy, he leaned against one of the few trees left standing, arms crossed over his chest, and watched her from over his sunglasses. An appreciative smirk lifted one corner of his mouth, and he said in the smoothest voice possible, "You're grounded."

She laughed and jumped into his arms.

"Yeah, yeah," he said, pretending not to enjoy the embrace.

When she finished, she turned full circle to take them all in again. "I can't believe I didn't recognize you. Especially you," she said, singling Garrett out, her white teeth blinding him, her smile was so big.

"Why me?" he asked and beckoned her to him. He took full advantage and kept her in his arms even longer this time.

"Because I've drawn you the very most."

"I've never seen any drawings of me."

"Oh, that's because I give them to—"

"Would you look at the time," Marika said, interrupting her. She lifted her wrist.

"You're not wearing a watch," he said.

"I just meant that we still have a creature to hunt down and shoot to death."

"She's right," Robert said. "We need to get back out there. We have to find that creature."

"That creature? You mean Hayal?"

Garrett tore his focus away from Marika. "Is Hayal twenty feet tall with black horns and razor-sharp claws?"

"Yes," Elwyn said, her expression grim. "Well, not twenty."

"And you know him?"

"Yes. He's my fiancé."

* * * *

By the time they got back to the compound, Cookie and the Loehrs were waiting outside and, quite literally, wringing their hands.

Before Robert had even come to a full stop, Cookie rushed to the SUV and, one could argue, dragged the child out of the car and into her arms. "Oh, my goodness," she said, swaying with the poor girl practically dangling from her embrace.

Elwyn laughed, as did Marika. She could hardly believe the events of the last couple of days. If she wrote a fantasy novel about it, an editor would say it was too outlandish. No one could suspend belief that much.

Cookie finally set her down and let the Loehrs embrace their granddaughter. Mrs. Loehr cried, her soft gray eyes a sea of emotion. While graying at the temples, Mr. Loehr still looked as dashing as he had the first time Marika met him four years ago when Garrett brought Zaire to the compound for his and Elwyn's first playdate.

They walked Elwyn inside, not ready to let go of her. The rest of Team Beep followed.

An hour later, as they sat around the dinner table, Elwyn couldn't get enough of drinking them in. Marika couldn't imagine what she'd been through. She'd grown up in a different dimension, on a different plane. Terrifying in its own right, but how did she get there in the first place?

They all had so many questions, but to everyone's credit, they kept them to themselves. At least for the time being.

Elwyn had showered, and Cookie found her some clothes. She was incredible at guessing sizes and made astonishingly good fashion choices considering her own attire bordered on manic with a sprinkle of colorblindness.

The girl was so lovely. No one could stop staring at her, including Marika. The scars on her face did nothing to subdue the beauty she'd become. But Marika was biased.

She still wore the bracelet that Osh had given her. Tarnished and covered in blood, it had survived what appeared to be years in a seemingly hostile environment.

"Where are Amber and Quentin?" Elwyn asked after she got a few bites into her. Amber was Cookie's daughter, though Quentin was a little harder to explain. Marika had always thought of him as a stray they'd taken in after a demon had possessed him and left him homeless.

"They're on their way home," Cookie said. "They wanted to be here sooner, but they were in the middle of finals. I forbade them from coming back until they took—and passed—every single test."

"They're still at university?" Elwyn asked. "They must be getting their doctorates by now. I want a doctorate someday. Maybe in ceramic sciences. Or manga. And what about Zaire?" She looked at Marika. "I can't wait to see him. Is he here? I bet he's taller than I am now."

An awkward silence followed her statement when everyone at the table realized at the exact same time that Elwyn didn't know. She had no idea that she'd only been gone a few days on Earth. The same thing had happened to Charley when Elwyn was a baby.

"Elwyn," Robert said, his mouth forming a grim line, "we don't know how long you've been gone on the other plane. We called the doctor to take a look at you and hopefully shed some light on your age, but we're guessing you're somewhere around fourteen?" He looked at

Cookie.

She agreed with a nod. "Yes. I'd say thirteen or fourteen."

Mrs. Loehr nodded as well. "That would be my guess, too. I would've said twelve, but only because you're so small."

Elwyn put down her fork. "Oh." She glanced down to study herself. "I'm sorry."

"Oh, honey, no." Mrs. Loehr leaned over and gave her granddaughter a hug. "You're gorgeous."

She pasted on a smile, unconvinced. "Has it not been seven or eight or nine years here?"

"Sweetheart," Garrett began, his expression just as grim as Robert's, "for us, you've only been gone three days."

Elwyn blinked, letting the concept sink in. Then she stood and walked to the window overlooking the plains with the mountains in the background. After a few moments, she sat back down. "So, Zaire is still only five?"

Marika nodded, but she hadn't expected the mischief on the girl's face. "Good. That means I can beat him up. Finally."

They laughed, but Marika wasn't wholly convinced that her light-hearted acceptance was genuine. Still, that could wait.

Now that the hard part was out of the way, Mr. Loehr asked, "Ellie Bug, how did you end up in another dimension?"

The girl took another bite of her taco, a delicacy she'd once described as structurally bothersome yet strangely addictive, and said, "I went there."

"But how, honey?" Robert asked.

"Like always. Only I couldn't find my way back this time."

Marika kept a close eye on Garrett. That cocktail may have worked wonders, but he'd still almost been killed. She handed him one of her tacos. When he questioned her by quirking a brow, she said, "I'm full. You'll have to eat that one for me."

He shrugged and carried on. "Okay, let's pretend that we don't know how you're able to space travel."

Elwyn giggled at that thought, but the description hadn't been far off the mark.

"If you want to go from point A to point B, what exactly do you do to get there?"

She looked at him as though he were daft, then said, "Through the portals," right before taking another crunchy bite.

He leaned back, as did Robert. "Right. The portals. And those are?"

She swallowed, took a drink of black coffee, then said, "The departed."

"The what?" Donovan asked, deciding to join in on the conversation. "The dead people?"

"Yes. That's how I've always done it, only I figured out—"

"Wait," Robert said, his mind completely blown according to his stunned expression. "The departed? You jump through the departed?"

She took another bite then nodded as Robert and Garrett put their heads together, literally, and talked quietly.

They straightened and then Robert said, "I've never heard of such an ability, and I'm old. Like millennia old. How is that even possible?"

"I don't know. I just figured out how to do it when I was a kid."

"So, like…yesterday," Garrett said.

"I guess. It's your fault."

He appraised her with an incredulous stare. "*My* fault?"

"Yes. We were playing hide and seek. I don't know if you remember this, but I always won."

"She did," he said, confirming the fact to everyone at the table.

"That's because I was trying to hide one day, and I kind of accidentally jumped through a departed."

"Accidentally?" Cookie asked. "How old were you?"

"I'm not sure. Maybe three? That first time scared me, though. I ended up in the woods at night, and I didn't do it again for a long time. Like a whole week."

"You used to end up in my office all the time," Garrett said, thinking back. "Even though I locked it to keep you out."

"Yep." She beamed at him, quite pleased with herself.

"You know what?" Eric said, his lean face full of contemplative thought. A dangerous thing for him. "I've experienced some crazy shit from you guys over the years, but a girl who can jump from dead person to dead person? I think that takes the cake. One of those pineapple upside-down things."

He got up to grab another beer. Apparently, that's what the guys did after such an ordeal, no matter the time of day, since it was barely one in the afternoon. He handed Garrett a bottle, too.

Garrett twisted the cap off then asked her, "Do you remember what you said to me just before you…what do you call it?"

She frowned. "I don't know. I never thought about it. It's like two pieces of a puzzle that I have to put together to be able to go through them."

He shook his head. "How do you fit them together?"

She shrugged by lifting a brow. "I just do."

"That's okay. Do you remember the last thing you said to me?"

After finishing off her second cup of coffee, she lifted a slim shoulder. "I said I'd find him."

"Find who?" Michael asked.

"Osh'ekiel." She said his name like it was a poem and absently cradled the wrist sporting her bracelet.

"You went looking for him?" Garrett asked, his smooth voice not the least bit condescending.

She only nodded, then added, "I never found him."

"I have something for you." Marika handed her the Osh doll. She worried the girl, now that she was older, would toss it away, thinking it childish. But she gaped at it for a solid minute, playing with its hair and coattails, then hugged it to her.

When Elwyn looked up again, she saw another member of the team standing in a corner. Her face brightened. She shot to her feet and ran over to him.

"Holy shit," Garrett said beside Marika. "Is that who I think it is?"

"I forgot you've never seen him before. The one and only, Angel Garza. The most inappropriate flirt this side of heaven."

Chapter Nine

When you are with your best friend,
it doesn't matter whose idea it was
as long as your alibis match.
—Meme

Angel was a departed thirteen-year-old gangbanger. He'd died in the nineties and had the A-line shirt and thick bandana low over his eyes to prove it. The first time they'd met, he'd hit Marika with a, "How you doin'?" replete with a New York accent, even though he'd never stepped foot outside of Albuquerque, New Mexico. At least while he was alive. She'd been a bit in love with the little shit ever since.

She felt positively giddy as Elwyn ran into his arms. And a tad jealous. Humans could rarely touch the departed, but Elwyn's mother and father could, thus the ability had been passed down to her.

"You grew up," Angel said to her, taken aback.

"Are you mad?"

"Never. I'm just sad I couldn't be there for you. I looked everywhere."

"I'm sorry."

"It's not your fault, *mi reina.*" My queen. Marika sighed. He ran a finger along the scar across Elwyn's cheek.

She covered it with her hand self-consciously. "It's ugly."

He removed her hand and replaced it with his own. "You are the most beautiful being I've ever seen. A tiny scar doesn't change shit."

Ever the poet, that kid.

Elwyn sank against him, and Garrett leaned over to Marika. "Should I be worried?"

"Yes," she answered. "With anyone else, no. But we are talking about Angel, who is as solid to Elwyn as you and I are."

"So, exorcism tonight?"

"The sooner, the better."

Elwyn brought Angel to the table and sat back down. Garrett nodded to him.

"Oh, that's right," Angel said, taking him in. "You can see me now. Guess I'll have to watch what I say around you then."

"Might be a good idea."

"Did you find him?" Robert asked Angel.

The Casanova shook his head. "He may be up in the mountains."

"Yes, which is why we sent you there to find him."

"I was headed that way when I was ambushed."

"Ambushed?" Elwyn asked, genuine concern on her face.

"Seems we have another beast running around. This one is smaller, but no less mean. Like a *pendejo* badger or something. He sent me packing with barely a word. It was more like a growl, actually."

"Oh, yes." Elwyn deflated. "He's been following me, too. For several worlds now."

"Following you?" Garrett said. "Sweetheart, why don't you explain everything from the beginning? I get how you jump from departed to departed now. Kind of. But how did you leave this plane?"

"Well, I knew Osh'ekiel wasn't on this one, so I decided to look on some others. Only then, I couldn't find my way back. There are so many." Her gaze slid past him to another place. Another time.

Robert nodded. "There are as many dimensions as there are stars in our universe."

"So, a lot," Eric said, helpfully.

Garrett sat stewing in a roiling sea of confusion. He just wanted to wrap his head around everything. Elwyn was the daughter of two gods. Was she automatically a card-carrying, secret handshake god? How did one get into the god club, anyway? Or maybe she was a demigod. How would that work?

She seemed to have completely different abilities from either of her biological parents. Like healing with her blood. Charley could heal with a simple touch and even bring people back to life. Or using the departed as a portal for interdimensional travel. Charley was the opposite. She *was* a portal, one that led to heaven, so those who didn't cross when they died could when they were ready.

And Reyes…well, he was the ultimate enigma. He and Charley could dematerialize and appear anywhere on Earth, but Reyes, a portal in his own right, albeit one to hell, could exist on both dimensions simultaneously. Beep, as far as anyone knew, couldn't. Why would their abilities be so different?

"It's like looking through a kaleidoscope," she continued, her mind far away. "And trying to find just the right pattern."

Mrs. Loehr took Beep's hand. "I'm so sorry, honey."

"It's my own fault, Grandma."

"No," Mr. Loehr said. "It's not. You were given extraordinary abilities when you were born. It was too much, too soon. Too big a bite. From what I understand, your biological mother's abilities came to her over time. She wasn't just handed the keys to the kingdom. She was given one room at a time to explore and learn before offered another. And she had Reyes to help her navigate, not us bumbling, fumbling humans."

A bubble of laughter escaped Beep. "I love my bumbling, fumbling humans."

Mrs. Loehr had to turn away and wipe her eyes.

"Where did you go?" Garrett asked. "And how did you end up with the fiancé from hell?" He didn't want to push her, but they did need to know what was going on and how to stop it.

"Oh, he's not from a true hell dimension," Elwyn said with a snort. "The Nepaui just like to think they are. But I've been to a few true hell dimensions. You do *not* want to go there."

"Wait," Marika said, "how many dimensions have you been to?"

"I don't know. I lost count around one hundred."

"And you jump through the departed there, too?"

"Yes. Turns out, the departed are everywhere. Sometimes, they are sentient beings. Other times, they're more like ferns. Or begonias. Not all of the pieces always fit. Sometimes, I have to take the long way around to get to a dimension I can almost make out."

Marika had a little drool on the corner of her mouth, she was so fascinated. Garrett handed her a napkin. She took it, glared at him, then asked, "Was there life everywhere you went?"

"Oh, yes. There is no death without life. I cannot enter a dimension that does not contain the departed in one form or another."

"Fascinating."

"Right? One place I went to was all water. The entire dimension. I didn't even know it at first because it wasn't like our water. It was much thicker. Like baby oil. But once I figured out how to breathe, it was amazing. Then I went to this one where the air was acid. It was horrible. I do not recommend that one. Then I found one that my mother had been to. A hell dimension with wraiths named after coffee drinks."

"Yes," Cookie said, excited. "Your mother named them."

"You got out of it?" Robert asked, astonished. "Even your mother couldn't do that, and she can—could—dematerialize."

"I did, but only because I used a wraith to unlock the next dimension. I believe her name was Salted Caramel Macchiato, but don't quote me on that."

Garrett raked a hand over his short hair. "This is all so incredible."

"But you want me to get to the point?" she asked.

"I want to hear everything. But right now, I need to know why that thing is on this planet and how to kill it."

"I told you. You don't."

"Beep," he said, getting frustrated. "Have you seen this thing? I mean, maybe it's grown since coming here."

"I doubt it. You described Hayal perfectly. Would you like to hear how I know?"

Marika snorted beside him. He almost glowered at her, but the sound was so cute he couldn't bring himself to sour her mood. "I would love to hear it."

She stood, refreshed her coffee, then sat back down. Cookie beamed at the girl, her pride in the girl's coffee-drinking prowess absolute. He fought a grin, trying not to encourage her.

"Okay, I ended up in a...well, a country for lack of a better word called Napau. And I was captured immediately by these huge creatures with horns and long, steely claws."

"That's them," Garrett said, his stomach contracting with the image.

"How old were you then?" Marika asked.

"Not much older than when I left."

"You were just a baby," she whispered. Absently, she took hold of Garrett's hand. He laced his fingers with hers.

"Long story short, I became a slave. But I accidentally saved my *castern*, my keeper, from an attack one night. That's when she realized that while I might be small, I could fight. She sent me to train with her sister."

"A slave?" Mrs. Loehr asked.

"Don't worry, Grandma. I could've left anytime. I could've jumped through any one of a thousand departed. But by that point, I was just so tired and lost."

Mrs. Loehr pressed her hands to her mouth.

"It was the first place where I felt like I could rest. Apart from all the training. And fighting. And maiming."

"Let me get this straight," Garrett said. "You fought them? Those creatures?"

"Often. I became their champion, and I caught the eye of the prince. He asked his father for my hand in marriage since I had no one to give consent. The king agreed. I did not."

"You turned him down?" Cookie asked.

"Which," Eric said, chiming in, "thank God. I mean, how would you even—?"

"As you were saying," Robert said before giving Eric a disapproving glare. "You turned him down?"

"Yes, but it's the law. Since I turned him down, we had to fight to the death."

Mrs. Loehr almost passed out. Mr. Loehr caught her and helped to steady her. He nodded for the conversation to continue without them while he took his wife upstairs.

"Okay," Garrett said once they were gone. "You had to fight him?"

"Yes. To the death." She bit her bottom lip. She only did that when she didn't want to admit to something. "The problem was, I didn't kill him. And now, he has to hunt me until the stars burn out. Either I have to finish the job, or he has to kill me. He can't go back home until he honors his house, though his reputation may never recover."

Cookie glanced around the table. "And we care about that? Are we caring about that?"

"No, sweetheart," Robert said.

"What I did was actually very cruel, though I didn't mean it that way." Elwyn glanced at Cookie as though seeking approval. Or forgiveness.

"Of course, you didn't," Cookie said. "You were trying to spare him."

"Exactly. Instead, I ruined his life. If I had just killed him, he would've died at the hands of a champion. It would have been a good death."

"So, no kidding?" Angel asked, shaking his head. "You fought those things?"

"Yes."

"*Hijueputa.*"

"When I didn't kill him, I ran to the nearest departed, right there on the battlefield, and just took my chances. I didn't think he'd be able to follow me, but he's right there every time I jump. I can't figure out how he's doing it."

"Can we get back to the part where you two were going to be married?" Eric said.

"No," the entire table said in unison. Then Garrett asked, "Any idea why he went after Marika?"

Elwyn's gaze darted to the subject at hand. "After you?"

Marika nodded.

"No. Unless… Were you carrying this?" She held up the Osh doll.

"Yes. In my bag."

"That could be why." She put the doll to her face and inhaled. "The doll smells like me. Hayal was after me and caught my scent. I'm so sorry, Marika."

"Don't be silly." She squeezed Garrett's hand. "It wasn't your fault."

"Of course, it was. All of this is my fault. Wait. He didn't scratch you, did he? Hayal?"

"No, but he did—"

"Any tips on how to capture the creature? How to kill it?" Garrett asked, cutting Marika off.

"Oh." Elwyn straightened her shoulders as though surprised by his question. "I apologize. I should have finished my statement earlier. He's my fiancé. Thus I have to be the one to kill him." Everyone stilled, so she quickly continued. "It's okay. He won't be my first. Sadly. Sometimes I had little choice. There is an old saying on that world. Kill or be killed."

Robert smiled. "We have something very similar here."

"I just don't understand how you fought them," Cookie said. "You're tiny."

"But fast," Elwyn said, a smile widening across her impish face. A visage that was at once familiar and strange and hauntingly beautiful. Garrett had known she'd be gorgeous. He did not expect the enchanting creature before him. Especially at the age of fourteen. Or somewhere thereabouts. Kids these days.

"And the other one?" Angel asked. "The smaller one who followed you here?"

"Did you get a look at it?" Her face lit up with hope.

"Not really."

"Fudge," she said, pouting her lower lip. The whole table chuckled.

That was the only curse word the Loehrs allowed her to use, but they had to make it feel like it was truly scandalous. So for a few months after Beep turned four, everyone would...slip and say the word *fudge* in front of her. Whoever was nearby would scold the loose-tongued devil for cursing in front of a child, and said child, naturally, started using the word as frequently as possible. It worked like a charm, and that was when Garrett knew what he was dealing with. The Loehrs were mad geniuses.

"Like I said," Angel continued, "he looked almost human, but not enough to pass as one in public. At least from the half-second glance I got."

Robert took a sip of the beer he'd been nursing for the last hour. "He's been following you through the portals, too?"

"I'm not sure. I just know he's been on my tail for the last few dimensions. How he's getting there, I don't know."

"I can't believe," Marika said, her gaze traveling the length of Beep, "that you grew up in another dimension. In several dimensions, in fact."

"Puts a whole new twist on foreign exchange student," Eric said with a snort.

That one wrenched a smile out of pretty much everyone. Except for Angel, who looked ready to blow up the world. Then again, maybe he always scowled like that. Since he'd never actually seen him before, Garrett had no way of knowing.

A faint look of alarm crossed Beep's face, but he couldn't imagine what she'd been through. He chalked it up to a bad memory, one he hoped she'd tell him about someday until she stood abruptly and started clearing the table.

That small act served as a cue for everyone to pick up their own plates, take them to the kitchen, and rinse them off—per house rules. The little explorer rinsed hers first and then made a beeline for Garrett's office. Curious, he followed her.

Robert hadn't missed the expression on her face either. He trailed right behind, and he and Garrett exchanged glances as they walked into the office. Decorated in heavy woods with gray accents, it sat in the back of the main house, close enough to the wooded area out back to have a gorgeous view, and close enough to the kitchen to be downright handy.

Beep stood in front of a framed map of the compound, a birthday gift from Cookie.

"This area is beautiful," Elwyn said to them, not bothering to turn around.

Garrett's chest tightened when he got a really good look at her frame. Far too thin with dark circles under her eyes, he didn't doubt for a moment how impossibly hard the last few years must have been for her. To be lost and completely alone on top of that. The thought was almost too much for him to bear, and guilt assaulted him on a whole new level.

He should have figured out what was going on before it'd come to what it did. It was his job to watch her every move. To know her every thought. To try and predict her every step. She was a child with powers beyond belief. This thing could've ended up so much worse.

It still might, come to think of it.

"You have no reason to feel guilty," Elwyn said to him, keeping her eyes on the map.

"I don't," he lied. "And how did you know?"

"You make faces when you think no one is looking." She grinned and pointed to a decorative mirror on the wall beside her. The one in which she could see him clearly.

"Cheater," he said.

Both he and Robert strolled up to her, flanking her to also look at the map.

"What's up, pumpkin?" Robert asked.

"Hayal is close."

Garrett tensed, and he was certain Robert did, too. "How do you know?" he asked.

She raised her face heavenward and drew a deep breath in through her nose. "I can smell him."

Garrett couldn't help it. He turned his head and sniffed, too. Nothing out of the ordinary. It must be another of her gifts.

"How close?" Robert asked.

"Three miles. Maybe four."

"And you can *smell* him?" Garrett asked. "From that far away?"

"I lived with them for many years. I could smell him from twenty miles away. But this is bad."

"Why?"

"If I can smell him, he can smell me. He knows I'm here. He will come for me."

"Let him," Robert said, putting a hand on her shoulder.

"I cannot risk it. I brought him here. He's my problem."

Garrett stepped to the side to look at her, but she wouldn't make eye contact. "He is *our* problem, Elwyn."

She lowered her head until her hair blocked his vision of her oval face. "No. I must leave."

"I forbid it," Robert said.

She turned at last, and they could both see the emotion glistening in her eyes. "You could not stop me if I wanted to go."

Robert raised his chin a notch. "I know, but I still forbid it. We'll do this together."

"We'll set a trap," Garrett said. "He'll never see us coming."

"Yes," she said with a breathy giggle. "He will."

"Well, then, we'll just have to be really smart about it."

After taking a few moments to think it over, she straightened her shoulders, agreed with a curt nod, then threw her arms around both of them in the best group hug Garrett had ever been in.

Chapter Ten

Just think…
Somewhere out there someone is thinking of you,
trying to figure out how to make your death look like an accident.
—Motivational Poster

After lunch, Marika called her mother and talked to Zaire. He asked about Beep, but that would definitely take some explaining, so she told him she'd fill him in the next day.

They sat up for hours throughout the afternoon and into the night, eating everything in the kitchen and listening to Elwyn's stories.

Every so often, Garrett left to consult with their security team on this or that, or Robert would take a call from their accountant or banker or decorator—the last one being the most ridiculous. It was all very clandestine, but she knew the troops were fortifying the barricades, and she had to wonder if the ruse was for her alone. If so, they needn't have bothered.

True to her former self, Elwyn apparently didn't need much sleep. Even now. And her stories were the stuff of both dreams and nightmares. The different forms of life she had seen. The food she'd tasted. The worlds she'd explored.

If Marika didn't know better, she'd have sworn she was in a coma somewhere, dreaming it all. It was so surreal. She was now part of the elite. A tiny portion of the population privy to the information in this room.

At a little after two in the morning, Garrett gestured humorously for Marika to look at Elwyn. Sure enough, when the girl crashed, she crashed hard. She'd passed out on the sofa in the great room, her pixie face turning absolutely angelic, one arm and one leg dangling haphazardly over the edge. It was adorable.

Donovan was asleep in the great room as well. He'd passed out on an overstuffed chair after everyone else had gone to bed.

Artemis decided to make an appearance just as they were about to carry Elwyn upstairs. Only Elwyn and the Loehrs lived in the main house, along with the housekeeper and the cook. Everyone else had his or her own cottage, with the biggest of those belonging to Garrett.

But he did have a nice sofa in his office here in the back of the main house that would accommodate her nicely. There were also at least two fully furnished guest rooms that Marika knew about. Still, she hadn't exactly been invited to sleep over, and she wondered if that was because everyone assumed she'd be sleeping with Garrett.

Not likely.

Artemis sat panting near Garrett's feet. He stood to gather up Elwyn but then stopped and said, "I can't believe I can finally see them."

Marika stood as well. "I'm glad you're not mad about it. It will take some getting used to."

"I think I can handle it." He reached down to pet Artemis. She got excited, a little too much, and jumped up.

Normally, since she was incorporeal, that would not be a problem. But since Garrett was so new to it all, he stumbled back and tripped on a lamp. It crashed to the floor with all the explosive bravado of a thousand thunderstorms. In his defense, he did try to catch it on his way down. He missed. Of course, that could've been chalked up to the fact that he'd almost died not twenty-four hours earlier.

Marika knelt down to him as he moaned in agony. "You can *see* them," she said, fighting a grin. "You can't *touch* them, Einstein."

He climbed to his feet and brushed himself off. "Just when I was starting to like you."

His words made her heart clench, a fact that annoyed her beyond measure. He was not taking her moratorium seriously at all.

That aside, he hadn't been kidding. The kid slept hard. She didn't even flinch when the lamp crashed. The Loehrs, unfortunately, did. They rushed downstairs, only to find a broken lamp on the floor.

"I'm so sorry," Marika said, searching the utility closet for a dustpan.

Mrs. Loehr shooed her aside. "It's okay, sweetheart. I'll get that if you and Garrett will get Ellie Bug to bed."

"You got it, Mrs. Loehr." Garrett bundled the elfin into his arms. "She weighs like two pounds. How can she fight anything other than a pesky gnat?"

"Do you think she's awfully malnourished?" Marika asked, following him. Unable to resist, she brushed back the girl's hair and kissed her forehead before he made it to the stairs. "There's no telling what she had to eat on all of those worlds. We live in this universe on this planet for a reason. It has everything we need to survive. To meet our nutritional needs."

"True." Mid-step up the stairs, he turned back to look at Donovan.

To the biker's credit, he hadn't flinched when the lamp fell over either, but that was probably the beer's influence.

"The doc will be here tomorrow," Garrett said, continuing up the steps.

"Do you like her?" Marika asked point-blank, not that she had a chance with Garrett. She just wanted to know.

"I adore her. When she's not jumping through dead people, that is."

"No, I mean the doctor."

"Oh. Yeah, sure, I guess."

Of course, he did. She was gorgeous. At least now she knew. "Is this hurting your back?"

"Not at all. It's probably eighty percent healed by now."

"Garrett, how is that possible?" she asked, rushing to his side now that they were on the landing.

"I told you. We have a secret weapon."

"Does it have anything to do with a certain little god and the fact that her blood heals?"

"Maybe. But what makes you think it heals humans? Maybe it only heals hellhounds."

"That would be pretty specific." She ran ahead and opened the door to Elwyn's bedroom. Thankfully, it had a full bed because there was a massive Rottweiler sprawled across it.

"I take it they share?"

Garrett chuckled. "'Parently."

She pulled back the covers and watched as Garrett, with the gentlest of movements, tucked the fully-clothed girl into bed.

"She's so beautiful," Marika said, still utterly in awe of the new teen.

Garrett kneeled down next to her and brushed a thick lock of inky black hair off Elwyn's face. "I have to admit, I can't get over the fighting thing. That boggles even *my* mind, and I've been in the know for many years."

"I just can't imagine how she could bring one of those creatures down, much less dozens. And she had to have begun when she was still a child." When he lifted a questioning brow, she added, "A smaller child. Who, apparently, sleeps like the dead."

"Yeah, when she sleeps."

Garrett had held his temper all afternoon and well into the night, but that was about to change. Now that he had the hellion all to himself, he planned to give her a piece of his mind then send her packing. Except, he was the one who'd brought her to the compound. He would have to give her a piece of his mind, not that he had many to spare, then take her home himself. It would be an uncomfortable drive back, but quite frankly, he didn't give a damn.

He stood and led Marika to the door. After one last look at the only being on the planet he would give his life for, besides his son, of course, he closed the door and started down the steps.

"I'm going to sleep on the sofa as long as Donovan doesn't snore too loudly," Marika said.

"We need to talk."

"Oh?" she asked, her voice tinged with a hint of surprise. "About?"

"Outside."

"I love the outdoors. Was that it?"

"You're funny." He took her by the elbow once they reached the first floor and led her out the front door into the cooling breeze of the New Mexico night. She couldn't help but notice two armed security guards walking the perimeter of the compound.

"It's lovely out," she said, her stomach filling with butterflies.

When he turned toward her, his face the definition of rage-filled—or hormonal, it was hard to tell—she started to contemplate her chances of hitching a ride away from the boonies in the middle of the night. Because she had a strange sensation that she was not going to like this conversation.

* * * *

Garrett looked across the moonlit compound at the adobe outbuildings, the Tuscan greenhouse, the area Beep insisted, before her vanishing act, would make the perfect spot for a pool. But more important were the people who lived here.

The creature was close, holding steady at almost three miles out. Beep had assured him not an hour earlier that Hayal was apparently going to wait until daybreak to attack.

"He is honorable," Beep had said to him during a third clandestine meeting that night, though the uncertain tone of her voice had given him pause. "Most of the time."

"Then again," Garrett had countered, "you did ruin his life. He could be feeling a mite vengeful at the moment."

"Yes. I *did*. I ruined his life. I just don't think he would attack a human."

Robert had been with them. He cast him a sideways glance full of admonishment.

Garrett had to agree. Why didn't he just tell Beep about the attack? Why keep it from her? Probably because she felt guilty enough about the whole thing. "What about when he went after Marika?" he asked, broaching the subject without giving away his secret.

"It had to be the scent. Perhaps"—she turned away in frustration—"perhaps he thought she was me?"

"Maybe," Robert said, doubt lining his face.

Considering everything that was happening, all he had to worry about, Garrett still seething over the events of the day, over Marika's actions, surprised even him. But he couldn't let it go.

He had never been a walking rage machine. It wasn't really in him. In fact, he'd often been called *laid-back* by many of his friends and colleagues. Easygoing. But the fury she'd ignited when she jumped in front of that spear—once it was all over, of course, and he'd gotten over the shock of almost losing her right then and there—kept eating at him.

He turned to her now, the anger he felt eating away at his insides springing forth. "Twice," he said from between clenched teeth. "You did that shit twice!"

Marika lifted her chin a visible notch. "If I did, I had a good reason. I'm certain of it. What are you talking about?"

"You don't know?" He advanced on her, and he could see by the tension coming to life in her slender body that she considered retreating. She didn't. She held her ground like a quaking deer waiting to be run down, as though it had a death wish. "Is that it? Do you have a death wish? Is that why you risked your life not once but twice for me today? Even after I told you after the first time never to do it again?"

"Please." She brushed at her shirt. "Like I listen to you."

He took hold of her shoulders. "That's the problem!"

The look of horror on her face shook him out of his momentary slip of sanity. He dropped his hands and stepped back. "I'm—I'm sorry. I didn't mean—"

"Yes, you did." It was her turn to be angry. Her eyes flashed in the low light of the moon. Her jaw set. She strode up to him for the sole purpose of jabbing a well-manicured finger into his chest. "You have blamed me for everything from the common cold to world hunger, all because I tricked you into giving me a baby. Well boo-hoo. I never asked you to be a part of our lives."

She started to stomp away, toward the road no less, but then turned back to him, absolutely livid. "You act as though I've ruined your life, but it was your decision to intrude on ours. I was perfectly happy. I had my child, one that was prophesied when I was a child myself, and I wanted nothing more than to keep him safe. To raise him in a loving, nurturing environment. Not a broken one where the father is off throwing back brewskies with the boys while his son wonders why he isn't good enough. What he did wrong to alienate his own father so completely."

"Is that what you think?" Garrett asked.

"I'm not finished!" she said, apparently on a roll.

"You just can't handle it. It's too much. I've betrayed you to the very depths of your soul, and you just can't get past it. So, you walk out of our lives for a second time. After all the proclamations of love and commitment, you're suddenly gone. Fine. *Hasta la vista*, baby. But no." She raised her arms in frustration. "Even though you hate me to hell and back, you just have to be a part of our son's life if for no other reason than to make me pay on a bimonthly-and-every-other-holiday basis. Every time you pick him up, you make sure I know what a piece of shit I am. Well, let me tell you something, Mr. Asshat." She stepped closer and looked up until they were nose-to-nose. "I am not a piece of shit. I never was."

Chapter Eleven

The most beautiful stories
always start with wreckage.
—Jack London

She turned, and that time, she really did head for the road. The deserted road that would end up with her blood splattered across it before morning. It was simply too dark with too many turns and had absolutely no shoulder whatsoever. If a semi happened down it…

But it wasn't her impending doom that spurred him into action. It was, of all things, his father. At least, the memory of his father. Of what he'd done. How he'd almost broken Garrett's mother. But Garrett only had himself to blame for that.

He stalked after Marika, twirled her around, and planted his mouth on hers.

He could feel the wetness on her cheeks, and guilt burned a hole into his stomach. But he couldn't stop kissing her. She tasted like peppermint. Smelled like vanilla and paradise. Felt like heaven.

After a moment, she eased against him. Let him molest her mouth and her jaw and her neck. He tilted his head and kissed her again, deepening it with each exploration of his tongue, until he felt her pull back. It was inevitable. She was a tad miffed.

"Why are you doing this?" she asked, her breath hitching. She couldn't have hurt him more with a sledgehammer.

He pulled her against him, noticing that the guards had

conveniently left to check the outbuildings. "I'm sorry," he said, burying his face in her hair. "I'm so sorry. I don't care what you've done. How many men you've been with."

"I beg your pardon?" She stepped back. "How many men I've been with?"

"No, not in general."

"Well, good, because that would make you one hell of a hypocrite. Oh, wait…"

He clenched his jaw. "I meant, you know, while we were together."

She hauled back and socked him on the arm in frustration. "What in the name of Bondye are you talking about?"

"I saw you. I don't care. Not anymore. If I've realized one thing over the last few days, it's that nothing should get in the way when you really love someone."

"Well, good for you." She turned and started toward the road yet again.

He stood in shock for a solid minute and then jogged to catch up with her. "Wait. Where are you going?"

"Home."

"But I professed my love."

She snorted. "Yes. You've done that before if you'll remember. About twelve hours before you walked out on us. Not me, Garrett. *Us.*"

"Damn it, Marika, I saw you."

She whirled around, the rage on her face fairly difficult to miss. "You saw me what?"

He shoved his hands into his pockets and dropped his gaze. "I saw you with another man."

The astonishment in her expression when he looked up would've been comical if the situation weren't so dire. Seeing her in the arms of another man had cut him so deeply, he worried that he'd never recover.

"Tall? Slim? Shaved head? Ringing any bells?" When she thought back but didn't answer, he continued. "I was coming over for dinner that night, or did you forget?"

"My cousin Jonas from Haiti? I hadn't seen him in years. He surprised me. And, yes, I suppose I did jump into his arms, but—"

"You were hugging him and kissing on him."

"Like I do Zaire? Like I do Elwyn? He's my cousin. I was so excited to introduce you. I made a huge dinner, and we waited. And waited.

Because someone wouldn't take my calls. He was embarrassed for me, and there I sat, singing your praises. Telling him what a good father you were. And you just left?"

Garrett swallowed, remembering the pain the image evoked like it was yesterday. Because a similar one had haunted him his entire life. "I don't know what to say. I thought—"

"I know what you thought." She stepped closer, her voice cracking, when she added, "I know exactly what you think of me, Garrett. I'm done. From now on, you may only pick up and drop off Zaire at my mother's. And if you really do love me, if you love him, you won't even do that anymore. He doesn't deserve the heartache."

Marika started toward the road for the third time, and Garrett could feel the world swallow him whole. Or maybe he just wished it would.

He slammed his eyes shut. Listened to the sounds of the New Mexico desert around him. Hardly a day went by when he didn't wonder what she was doing. How she was coping with everything. If she liked her job. If she ever wished her life had turned out differently. She was the only woman on the planet he'd ever wondered that about. She was the only woman he'd ever had in his life that he cared enough about to *want* to know.

Did that make him a selfish dick? Probably. One thing was for certain, he was getting a T-shirt that read *Mr. Asshat* printed immediately. When the euphemism fit...

He didn't want to push her. Well, any more than he already had. But he did have to win her back before she became roadkill. Or worse, Hayal-kill. There was still a freakishly large alien running about, after all.

Unfortunately, he had a sinking feeling that the only way to win Marika back was with the truth. He tended to steer clear of it—of that particular one, anyway—as often as possible. But it was now or never.

He caught up to her and walked beside her as non-threateningly as he could. "The road into Pojoaque has no shoulder."

She ignored him.

"It's very narrow, with lots of curves."

She kept walking.

"You'll end up a hood ornament before dawn."

She stared straight ahead. Thankfully, it would take almost an hour to walk to the main road. The more dangerous one. That gave him an hour to change her mind.

Just as she was about to trip on a large rock on the side of the road, he grabbed her shoulders and steered her clear.

"How did you see that?" she asked. "Never mind."

He drew in a deep breath and dove in headfirst. "I am my father's son, as they say."

A vehicle approached them from behind. It rolled slowly over the gravel road, the faint glow of parking lights illuminating the grasses around them. Apparently, one of his security guards, Sadowski most likely, was following to keep an eye on things. He'd have to give him a raise.

"As to the topic of malfeasance number one, my mother tricked my father into marriage." He saw her shoulders tense, so he quickly explained. "I know that's not what you did. Nowhere near what you did. But it's what she did, and Dad never forgave her."

Talking had never been Garrett's strong suit. Talking about his parents…Well, he never talked about them. A concrete lump settled in his chest every time he did, but if anyone was worth that discomfort, it was the woman stalking away. Somehow, he knew if he didn't make things right, his opportunity would be lost forever.

"My father grew to despise her and never missed an opportunity to let her know it."

Garrett looked out over the moonlit landscape, purples and grays all around them. It was easier to focus on that than the topic at hand.

"He wasn't wrong, really. I come from a long line of con artists. Conning was in Mom's blood. Tricking a man into marriage, especially a well-off engineer, was old hat. But I think she really loved him. In her own way."

Marika kept walking, although her gait was less hurried now. Less angry.

"She began drinking more and more until she ran her car off a bridge into a deep ravine in Diablo Canyon." Garrett felt his throat close with the memory of that night. The cops knocking on the door. Their lights flashing red and blue through his bedroom window, reflecting off the walls around him. "They said it was an accident. It wasn't."

Marika slowed her steps but kept her gaze locked on the road ahead.

"But before my dad died, he turned his rage on me. I guess with my mother toasted most of the day, his words no longer affected her like they had. He needed a new target."

She slowed even more, her jaw set firmly in place, refusing to wipe away the tears shimmering silver in the moonlight.

"He didn't beat me or anything. Nothing as bad as that. Just made sure I knew what a burden I was. How he'd never wanted me. How my mother had used me to get him, meaning she'd never really wanted me either."

Marika stopped though still avoided his gaze.

"But what you have to understand is that he was wrong about her. Partly, anyway. She may not have wanted me at first, but she loved me."

Marika still didn't look at him when she asked, "Did he hurt you?"

"Nah." He twisted one of the skull rings on his finger. "He was just a dick. Called me every name in the book. Believe it or not, it's a very long book. But I eventually learned something about him."

She angled her face toward him but still refused to make eye contact. Instead, she watched him fidget with his ring. Suddenly self-conscious, he dropped his hands.

"I realized he became particularly belligerent after I accomplished something. Like when my little league team won first place and I brought home the trophy. Or when I won a race at school. Or when I scored the highest on a test. I was always trying to make him proud of me without realizing he couldn't be. He could never be proud of me. He didn't have it in him." Garrett looked at her from over his shoulder. "It took me years to figure out that at the root of everything he did was jealousy. He was simply jealous. Who's jealous of their own kid?"

She studied her palms in the low light. Rubbed at some invisible dirt there.

"Anyway, he died when I was ten, so none of it really matters. Which brings us to malfeasance number two. When I saw you in your cousin's arms..." He swallowed hard, trying to reopen his airway. "Barely a month after my dad died, I caught my mother in the arms of another man. I'd come home early from school, still grieving the loss of a man who didn't deserve it, and she had another man over. I saw them embracing through the window. I ran inside and called her all the names my father had called her all those years. Every hateful, belittling knife he'd cut her with came out of *my* mouth that day." He shoved his hands into his pockets. "She was dead six hours later."

Marika lifted a hand to her mouth and turned her back to him.

He angled away from her as well, the pain threatening to swallow him whole. "She just needed to be loved. Everyone needs to be loved and accepted. Not that any of that matters now."

She stepped in front of him and put a hand on his chest. "Of course, it does. But you just lied to me again."

He sank into the pale depths of her irises. "I promise I didn't."

"You did. He most definitely hurt you. He may not have hit you, not physically, but emotional scars run just as deep."

After a long moment where pain warred with desire, he asked, "Brewskies? Throwing back brewskies with the boys? That's the best you've got?"

She pressed her lips together.

"Can you forgive me?" he asked.

"For being an asshat?"

One corner of his mouth rebelled against the establishment and lifted despite his attempts to subdue it. "That's Mr. Asshat to you, love."

He brushed the wetness from her cheek with a thumb and bent to claim her mouth. Her lips were as soft as the rest of her. And felt just as good. Like morning dew after a hot rain.

She slid her hands up his chest and around his neck, then pressed her succulent body against his. He growled into the kiss, wrapped his arms around her and walked her back toward the SUV that had been following them.

He needed an anchor because he was about to do something she would never forget. He didn't know what yet, but it would come to him.

Sadowski got out of the SUV and stumbled over his words, saying something like, "Okay then, I'll just, you know, be over there."

The man had better be over there. Far, far over there. Garrett had shit to do.

He pressed her against the grill then leaned back. The lights cast a soft glow on her beautiful face. Her lashes were spiked with wetness. Her lips were already swollen from his efforts. And her chin, her adorable chin he'd nibbled on more than once during their rendezvous, quivered just a little.

Running his hands up the back of her shirt, he undid her bra and lifted both it and the shirt over her head. Goose bumps spread over her bare skin, and she clasped his head to her breast. He knelt in front of her, cupped her breasts in his hands, and circled one delicate nipple with his tongue until it hardened before seeing to the other.

He heard the blood rush through her veins. Saw the dilation of her pupils even under the cover of night. Smelled the pheromones waft off her silken skin like a potion. The combined efforts of her body's response to him sent him spiraling and he had to fight for control over his own. Something he hadn't had to do since puberty.

When he grazed his teeth over her, Marika gasped and pulled him closer, but he seemed to have other ideas. He trailed kisses down her stomach, and for all of ten seconds, she wondered how her night had taken such a drastic turn. First, they were fighting. Yet again. Then Garrett was opening up to her. Opening up! It was the most monumental thing to ever happen to her, apart from Zaire's birth. And both were just as painful.

But now. Now with his hands and his fingers and his mouth in all the right places, she was reeling. When he picked her up, carried her to the side of the SUV, opened the back door, and deposited her on the long seat, the leather startlingly cool against her bare back, molten lava pooled in her abdomen.

Barely able to see his face in the low light, she could just make out his strong jaw and full mouth. His straight nose and furrowed brow. His stern expression and intoxicating masculinity.

But the thing that took her breath away, that always took her breath away was the fact that his irises reflected the moonlight like it was made from it. Silvery and shimmering, they seemed to glow with drunken sensuality.

Moonlight did things to people, and his eyes did things to her.

He laid her back against the seat and peeled down her jeans, taking both them and her shoes completely off. They fell to the footwell with a soft thud, then he stopped. Seemed to bask in her image. Seemed to drink her in as though she were the whiskey he wanted to drown his sorrows in.

Her panties were next. They were really all she had left in the world. Her last line of defense. Once they were gone, she knew she'd be lost forever. Unfortunately, he was taking his sweet damned time about it.

His fingers slid under the elastic surrounding her legs. Tested it. Tugged at it. She wiggled her bottom, trying to get them off faster. He laughed softly, the sound deep and alluring as he took hold of her hips and forced her to still.

She may have growled.

Another deep laugh. Another slip of the fingers. Another tug. Then cool air washed over her lady bits. Her pulse pounded as he slid her panties down her thighs, over her knees, and past her calves, only to stop at her ankles. He twisted the tiny piece of material in his fist until her ankles were locked together. Then he raised them into the air with one hand and slid his long fingers inside her with the other, the coolness of his rings rubbing along her clit.

She heard a sharp intake of breath and realized it was hers. He dipped the length of two fingers, the pressure heady, before he pulled them out and brushed her own wetness over the folds of her cunt.

He untwisted the panties and kissed the inside of first her right ankle, then her left, his breath warm against her skin, and his scruff tickling it. Then he spread her legs apart, exposing her completely, and gently wedged one ankle between the seat back and the side panel and the other between the driver's side headrest and the back of the seat.

She lay completely spread eagle. He stopped to take her in, his heavy-lidded gaze grazing over every inch of her and causing the most incredible sensations to ripple through her.

She reached down and tugged at his shirt, wanting to see as much of him as he was of her. He obeyed, lifting the shirt over his head, but then stopped there. His impossibly wide shoulders tapered down to a lean waist. He ran his fingers along the inside of her knee, but she protested with a wiggle and a moan and pulled at the button of his jeans.

Without taking his eyes off her, he made quick work of the button and zipper and slid his pants past his hips and over his steely buttocks. His hard cock spilled out, and she wanted nothing more in that moment than to wrap her lips around it. But he had other plans.

He bent over her at last, the width of his shoulders spreading her even more, and covered her clit with his mouth, hot and wet and sensual. The soft sweep of his tongue teased and caused a swell of unimaginable pleasure. It pooled in her abdomen and reverberated out from there.

His tongue flitted, and his fingers probed, and it didn't take long before the promise of an orgasm spiked within her. She'd been ready for days. It was no wonder it didn't take long.

She dug her nails into his shoulders and stilled as much as she could, beckoning the orgasm forward, begging it to come closer. Her lungs seized, and the pressure between her shaking legs swelled as his tongue coaxed her to the very edge.

He opened her more, spreading the folds of her sex to give the very tip of his tongue access to the most intimate part of her. He sucked and stroked and worked another finger inside her until her hips rose off the seat, and the blistering heat of an orgasm rushed forth. The sweet sting of release exploded and washed over her in unimaginable waves. Each one a little higher than the previous. Each peak a little sharper.

She had yet to come down when she felt him push inside her, escalating her climax even more. He buried the hardness of his cock in one solid thrust and then waited like a predator watching its prey. His muscles coiled. His jaw clenched. His face the picture of sweet agony as he tried to hold back.

But her orgasm, still rippling through her, milked an orgasm out of him. He groaned. His muscles contracted. He grabbed the armrest on the door above her head, ripping it loose as his climax rendered him helpless.

When he let go of the armrest, and his frantic breaths calmed, she uttered one word between pants of her own.

"Two," she said, her voice barely audible.

He grinned down at her. "For reals? You came twice?"

She smirked and followed up her announcement with, "I win."

He laughed and collapsed on top of her, burying his face in her hair. Her second favorite place for his face to be.

Chapter Twelve

Real men won't break your heart,
they'll break your headboard.
—Meme

Garrett lay in utter abjection across the seat. Marika lay on top of him, their legs protruding out the door.

"What's wrong?" she asked him.

How could he tell her? How could he admit that he had come before he meant to? Although it wasn't exactly premature ejaculation, it may as well have been.

"Tell me," she coaxed, much like she'd coaxed an orgasm out of him before he was ready.

"It's nothing."

"Tell me," she said, her voice low and sweet.

He lifted a shoulder. "I had big plans. I was going to give you a night you'd never forget."

"Oh, I don't think I'll be forgetting this for a very long time."

"Promise?"

She giggled. "Promise. But I do have to ask. Did you say all of that about your parents just to get in my pants?"

"Yes."

"Well, it worked."

"It fucking rocked. Tomorrow I'm going to tell you about the time I accidentally killed Mojo, my eastern box turtle."

"Oh, no," she said, her voice full of mock concern. "How sad."

"Yeah. He died a horrible death."

"Hmmm."

"A chainsaw accident."

"Oh, my god. He died from a chainsaw?"

"No. His death was more chainsaw adjacent."

Garrett heard a voice and stilled. "Did you hear that?"

She waited and listened. "I don't hear anything."

He heard it again. Someone shouted from a distance, and it took Garrett about three seconds to be dressed and out of the SUV. He ran toward the main house, looking back to make sure Marika followed him. She ran while trying to get her shirt over her head.

It was Cookie. She rushed toward them, waving her arms frantically. When she was about ten feet away, she slowed, holding her chest from the effort.

He took her by the shoulders. "What is it, sweetheart?"

"She's gone," she said between huffs. "Elwyn is gone."

A shockwave rocketed through his body. "Did the creature—?"

"No," she said, almost hyperventilating. "She snuck out. We checked the footage. She crawled out of her window and headed toward the clearing."

"Son of a bitch. We had a plan. Why would she do that?"

"Because she's exactly like her mother."

"God help us." He turned to check on Marika again.

She was struggling to get into her shoes. The SUV they'd *borrowed* pulled up beside her. She waved Garrett on. "I'm good. Just go," she said before climbing into the vehicle.

"Me, too," Cookie said. "I'll catch a ride." She indicated the SUV with a nod. "Wait, Garrett. Please, just—"

"I know, sweetheart." He squeezed her shoulders reassuringly then took off at a dead run back to the house.

By the time he got there, predawn light was just piercing the horizon. Everyone was present and accounted for, scrambling to gather their weapons. Angel watched from a corner. He walked up to Garrett. "Where is she?" he asked the teen.

"In the clearing."

"You've been agitated since last night," Garrett said. "What's going on?"

"I don't think she told you the whole truth."

He'd been strapping a gun around his waist. He stopped. "What do you mean?"

"I'm not sure. I think she knows more about that creature than she's telling."

"I need you to be more specific."

"I think she went along with your plan to placate you."

"Fuck." Garrett raked a hand over his head. "She really is her mother's daughter."

"Identical. I think she's had her own plan the whole time. And I think the creature knows it."

He stilled at that, his hand pausing on the zipper of his duffle bag. "Why do you say that?"

"It's like he was waiting for her. Like he knew she would go to him because he didn't give her a choice."

"How did he manage to communicate that?"

"The hellhounds. You and Marika. He attacked so she knew he would. So that she wouldn't jump planes again."

"We need to move," Robert said just as Cookie and Marika burst into the house.

"I'm coming," Cookie informed him.

"Sadowski," Garrett said, nodding to the security guard.

The kid walked up to Cookie and indicated a chair at the table. "Sorry, Mrs. D."

"You're commandeering me?" she asked her husband, appalled. "I'm appalled."

"You can be mad at me later."

"Oh, it's far too late for that, *Mr. D.*"

He exhaled and said under his breath, "Great."

"Well, I *am* coming," Marika said, stabbing Garrett with a challenging scowl.

"Marika—"

"No. Don't you dare. You dragged me into this."

After a long moment where he conjured any number of ways to keep her here, he gave in. She did have a point. "Okay, but you have to put your bra on the *inside* of your shirt."

She gasped, looked down, then glared at him.

"I win."

"No, you don't. That was cheating."

"Duh," he said with a shrug, right before he handed her a nine millimeter semi-automatic. "You good with that?"

She hesitated, but only for a second. She checked the chamber and slipped it into one of Garrett's holsters.

"That belt won't fit you."

She buckled it around her waist, but it hung loosely at her side. "Good enough."

"Just don't try a quick draw."

"No worries. If I have to draw, it will be anything but quick."

* * * *

They raced across the rugged terrain, Garrett following Sadowski's SUV. A small army followed after him. Just as they came into a clearing about three miles from the compound, Sadowski's SUV slammed into something so hard, it lifted the backend of the vehicle off the ground.

Garrett skidded to a halt, jumped out of his truck, and ran toward the SUV. The others scrambled out and took up positions in a defensive formation as he checked on the kid. The airbags had blown, but Sadowski would be fine. Then he ran to the front to see what he'd hit.

Nothing. Absolutely nothing.

He waved away the smoke billowing from the engine and went to step around to the front when, just like the SUV, he slammed his shoulder into something. He blinked and patted the air. His hand landed on a cool, hard surface, smooth and invisible.

"What the fuck?"

Marika ran over to him. She lifted her hands, but he put an arm out to stop her.

"Don't touch it. It could be harmful." As far as he knew, it could cause brain tumors or hair loss. No telling what kind of radiation could be emitting from it as they stood there.

"What is it?" she asked.

"Some science fiction shit is what it is. It's a barrier of some kind."

"Like a forcefield?"

"Exactly."

He scanned the area and gestured with a nod. "That's why the hellhounds are pacing and pawing at the grass. They can't get in either."

"Look at Artemis." Marika pointed.

He saw her about half a click away. "She's completely incorporeal," he said, astonished. "How can she not get past it?"

"I don't know, but I don't like it."

He turned and scanned the inside of a huge circle where the barrier must have been if the hellhounds were any indication. A scattering of small trees dotted the area as well as several huge boulders. Beep stood from under a tree and walked over to them, spear in hand.

"Son of a bitch," he said under his breath.

"Oh, my god, Garrett," Marika said. "We have to get her out."

"I think that's what Artemis and the hounds are trying to do." He watched as the tiny girl he loved more than air walked up to them, her expression solemn, her eyes apologetic. "What are you doing here, sweetheart?" he asked her.

"I'm sorry. I had no choice."

"We always have a choice, baby."

Her expression was so sorrowful, it broke his heart. "Not this time."

Frustration strangled him. "What is this?" he asked, pounding his fist against the barrier.

"Nepaui elemental light. It is impenetrable. Hayal doesn't want me to get help from, well, you." She turned and scanned the interior of the dome. "Sadly, he is less honorable than I previously believed."

"You mean other than trapping a child inside this thing to fight her to the death all because he can't take rejection?" Garrett looked around. "That's what this is, right?"

She pursed her lips. "It doesn't matter."

"Stand back." He drew his sidearm and shot two bullets at the barrier. They bounced off without a trace. The material simply flashed iridescent then repaired itself.

Desperation began to take hold. He holstered his gun and asked, "Why did you leave? We had a plan."

"First, it wouldn't have worked. And second…second, I didn't want you to see this."

He put his hand on the transparent barrier. "See what, baby?"

Her chin quivered, and she looked away. "What I have become."

"Elwyn," he said, his voice hitching with a sob, begging her to be safe. To survive.

She grinned and put her hand on the other side of the shield, mirroring his, almost like they were touching. "You never call me by my name."

"I will call you anything you want if you'll just get me inside there. Please, baby."

"Will you call me Queen Salmon Patty?"

He tried to smile. He failed. "I will." He saw the beast uncurl from behind a boulder and felt his knees weaken. His chest rose and fell rapidly as though he couldn't catch his breath.

It slowly walked up behind her, in no hurry for the fight to begin. She bowed her head, as though accepting the inevitable.

Right before she turned, she met his gaze and whispered, "I love you."

Garrett broke down. He pounded on the barrier. It felt cold like glass, yet it gave—just barely—underneath his fist. He pounded harder, over and over, yelling at it to break.

Marika tried to pull him off. He stopped and watched what was about to happen as though it were in slow motion. The size difference was so great it was almost comical. A field mouse facing off against a grizzly.

"I'm sorry, Hayal," Elwyn said, seeming genuinely sad. "I didn't want it to end this way for you."

She was speaking English to it, but it seemed to understand.

It tilted its head as though sizing her up, pointed its spear at her, and said in stilted, guttural English from behind its blood-red mask, "You…haven't…won…yet…little girl."

"I'm sorry nonetheless."

Angel appeared beside them. Garrett panicked. Tried to grab him by the collar. His hand went straight through. "Get in there," he said, his voice a hiss. "She can jump through you. She can escape."

"I can't. I've tried." He pushed against the barrier. It was as solid to him as it was to Garrett. "It's blocking us from entering."

The creature turned to take up position, but Beep continued. "Please give my regards to your mother."

The beast whipped around. Whatever she meant by that, it definitely infuriated him. He charged forward, and Garrett's muscles seized.

Beep lowered herself to the ground and watched him from beneath her dark lashes. One second she was in front of him, readying to spring. The next, she was behind him, landing on the earth, whisper-soft.

Everyone looked on confused until they saw her spear lodged under the beast's chin, the tip sticking out from the top of its head.

Hayal stumbled then caught his footing, but only for a few stunned seconds. As Beep turned around to watch him, he fell forward like a tree falling to the ground.

He landed with a loud thud. Dirt billowed up around him and formed a cloud over his body.

"She moves like Charles," Garrett said, remembering Beep's mother and the first time he'd seen her move at the speed of light. Impossible for the human eye to track.

"She did it." Marika squeezed his arm.

Beep walked to the fallen creature. With one foot braced on its head, she grabbed hold of the spear and pulled the blood-soaked length of it out in one long heave. Then she turned to the now-empty field, her stance wide as though readying for another fight.

Garrett looked on confused until he saw a second creature materialize twenty feet in front of her, this one more humanoid, yet somehow wilder. He held two massive knives, one in each hand, curved and wicked. Created to kill.

"That's it," Angel said.

Garrett glanced between the two of them. "The creature that followed her?"

The teen nodded and pushed against the barrier again.

"Angel, what aren't you telling me?" At least this guy was smaller than the last one. Then again, the bigger they were…

"He's powerful," Angel said. "I could feel it when he passed by. Like the heat from a nuclear reactor."

Suddenly worried again, Garrett pushed against the barrier, too. Marika joined in, shoving with her shoulder. Robert, probably the only sane one, didn't bother. He just watched, his mouth set in a grim line.

They stopped when Beep sank low to the ground. Ready to spring into action again, she took her spear into both hands and pointed it at the intruder.

Her opponent's hands flexed on the knives. He watched her for a long moment, tilted his head as though studying her, then turned his back to her. In that same instant, she turned her back to him and

Garrett's heart got stuck in this throat. Then they waited. Beep coiled to strike, steady and low to the ground. The creature standing like he hadn't a care in the world.

"It's a demon," Robert said, frowning. "What the hell is—?"

"Wait. Those rocks." Garrett pointed to the boulders marking the boundaries of the barrier. Nine in all. No, ten. "I've never seen them before."

While they blended perfectly with the landscape, tan highlighted with golds and shadowed with darker browns, they were somehow the wrong size for the area. The wrong shape.

As Garrett and the team stood helplessly by, the rocks moved. Beep sank lower and the demon followed suit, his elbows out, his knives positioned perpendicular to the earth beneath him.

Suddenly, Beep's words about Hayal not being as honorable as she'd hoped made sense. Each rock transformed into one of the creatures. Another of the Nepaui.

Once they'd taken shape, they shook off the last remnants of whatever they had been.

"How can that come out of a small boulder?" Angel asked.

"There are ten," Garrett said to Robert. "You have to have a trick up your sleeve. You have to know something."

"This is new to me, too. I have no idea how to get in there. How to bring this down."

Before he finished, the battle began. Marika sank to her knees and covered her face, unable to watch. But Garrett couldn't have torn his gaze away if he'd been paid to. His lungs forgot how to work as the fight began anew.

Almost as fast as Beep, the demon sprinted toward one of them, scaled it in one giant leap, and sliced its throat before it could even react. Then he jumped onto the next one's back and dispatched it the same way.

By the time he got to the third, however, they were catching on. One of them sliced its claws through the air, shredding the demon's shoulder. But he didn't stop fighting.

Beep did much the same, only she moved even faster. Too fast for them to follow. Before they knew it, two of the creatures were falling to their deaths, their spines severed at the neck with her spear, but a third had caught hold of her. Her tiny body in its massive claws. She struggled to break free as it closed its fist.

The force would break her. Would crush her lungs and shatter her bones. The edges of Garrett's vision darkened, and the whole world tilted sideways until the beast let out an earsplitting scream. Beep fell to the ground. Buckets of blood followed in her wake as the creature held its severed hand.

The girl got her footing, then looked across the field. The demon took down another and had only two left. He slid between one's legs and sliced through its Achilles heel in much the same way Garrett had.

But the fifth one was waiting for him, its spear at the ready. As the demon slid out of the melee, the creature raised the spear.

Beep jumped to her feet and sent her spear flying. Her aim was so fast and true, the creature had no idea that he'd been killed by a spear through his skull. He sank to his knees just as a spear burst out of Beep's chest.

Garrett stood in disbelief for a solid minute, unable to make sense of the metal tip protruding from the beloved girl's sternum. It wasn't real. None of this was real. He heard someone yelling her name over and over, beating on the barrier with all of their might, and realized it was him.

Beep looked down, her face expressionless, and sank to her knees before collapsing in the wild grasses.

The demon made quick work of the one he'd disabled and looked toward the other side of the field. He stopped as though stunned, as shocked as Garrett, then bolted forward.

He threw the knives effortlessly. They spun like boomerangs and cut the throat of the one whose hand Beep had sliced through, the one whose spear had pierced her tiny chest. The knives spun back to him and he caught them easily as Garrett's fingers curled around Hayal's fallen spear.

He raised it and sent it flying across the field toward the last of the ten monsters. The one who'd raised his foot and was about to slam it down onto Beep's fragile body.

Without looking back, the demon ducked the deadly weapon as it sailed over his head, then he slid to a stop beside Beep. The spear flew true to Garrett's aim and impaled the creature dead center between its eyes. It stood frozen, as though in disbelief, for several agonizing seconds before it accepted its fate and fell straight back, landing with a loud thud.

Garrett turned toward Beep. Before he could stop the demon, it broke off the tip of the spear then pulled the shaft out through her back, wrenching an air-shattering scream from her.

"No!" Garrett yelled. She would bleed to death even faster.

He raced forward, but it was too late. Blood gushed like a geyser out of her chest. Garrett stopped and looked on in disbelief. The demon had kneeled down and gathered her, unconscious, into his arms.

Garrett's hand landed on his sidearm as he ran forward. His entire team followed, raised their weapons and trained them on the demon. All except Robert. He would never put Beep in danger. He walked onto the battlefield as though he'd done it a thousand times. He'd been an angel, however. Perhaps he *had* done it a thousand times.

Garrett motioned for the rest of his team to lower their weapons.

She wasn't breathing. Wasn't moving. The demon lowered his head and put his mouth on hers. He exhaled, and Beep's chest rose, but mouth-to-mouth would do nothing to stop the bleeding.

Garrett started forward again. Robert stopped him with a hand on his arm.

After a moment, the demon stood with her tiny body draped over his arms, watching them from behind a curtain of thick black hair.

"We need to get her to medical," Garrett said to him, straining to talk past the lump in his throat.

The demon stepped forward, keeping a wary gaze on them. The way he carried her, his every move as gentle as a summer breeze, spoke volumes. He'd been following her to help keep her safe. Only a fool would not be able to see that.

Garrett distanced himself a little more from the maddening crowds to ease the demon's concern.

Just as he got close enough to take her, Beep's eyes fluttered open.

Garrett looked down at her, his knees almost buckling, and thanked any and all higher powers for the odd placement of her organs. "You're lucky your heart is in the wrong place."

"Or in the right one," she said weakly, the barest hint of a grin lifting one corner of her pretty mouth.

He went to take her, and she grimaced through a bout of what he could only imagine was agonizing pain. The demon stopped and waited for her to recover before moving again.

When she did, she looked up at him and gasped softly. The gasp was followed by another grimace, but despite what it must've cost her, she lifted her hand to his face.

Confused, Garrett took a closer look. Then he blinked as recognition shocked him to his core.

Beep said the name they were both thinking, her voice whisper-soft and as fragile as butterfly wings. "Osh'ekiel."

He lowered his head, his expression unreadable.

It was him, but it wasn't. He was more demon and less human since their last encounter. Even so, Garrett recognized the angular shape of his jaw. The arrogant set of his chin. And the eyes. Before he looked away, he saw those deep bronze eyes that had always fascinated him. The things he must have seen over the centuries.

Robert stepped closer just as Osh handed Beep over to Garrett.

"Osh," Robert said, as stunned as the rest of them.

The minute the girl was out of his bloodied arms, Osh stepped back and slowly dematerialized, soaking in the image of Beep one last time before disappearing entirely like sand on a breeze.

Garrett looked down. The little hellion was unconscious again, so he could move more freely. The hellhounds and Artemis wanted to check on her personally, but they didn't have time. Despite their whimpers, Garrett jogged to the truck with Beep where Marika and Eric waited with a medical kit. They put her in the back on a blanket and pressed on the wound in her chest.

"How did you do that?" Marika asked him.

He lifted her into Eric's waiting arms, and asked, "What?"

"You…you broke the barrier." She grabbed the medical kit and tore it open.

He jumped into the truck and helped Eric place her on a tarp as Donovan and Robert jumped in, too. Donovan tore open Beep's shirt while Robert applied pressure to her wound even though the bleeding had slowed drastically.

"How did you do that?" Marika asked again, handing Robert a gauze pad. "You broke through it. The barrier. You brought it down."

Garrett glanced up, but only for a second, just long enough to realize everyone was staring at him like he'd grown an extra head.

"No. It just vanished."

"After you broke it," Robert said. He seemed impressed.

"Well, I have no idea what happened. Eric, can you drive?"

"You got it." He jumped out of the truck, wiping blood onto his jeans, and hurried to the driver's side.

"Where are we taking her?" he asked over his shoulder.

Robert answered. "To medical. We can't take her to a hospital."

"What?" Marika asked, stunned.

"It's okay, hon," Garrett said. "She's already healing."

She looked down and nodded, not completely convinced.

Eric drove as fast as he could without jostling his precious cargo too much. Beep remained unconscious the whole way, her body using all of its energy to heal, but she did ramble every so often on the way back.

"Osh'ekiel," she said in her sleep.

Marika took her hand and squeezed.

Beep smiled. "He found *me*."

Chapter Thirteen

You only need to find yourself.
Everything else can be Googled.
—Meme

"It's definitely blood," the doc said, handing the bracelet back to Robert. "See those?" she pointed to several tiny, elongated beads. "Those aren't beads. They're vials filled with blood. His, I'm assuming."

"Osh used the bracelet to track her," Robert said. "To be able to keep an eye on her from anywhere. That's why he made it."

"But where has he been?" Garrett asked.

"I don't know yet."

"Hell," Beep said, still weak, her voice hoarse. It had only been a few hours since they got back, but she'd lost a ton of blood before she began to heal. And she was tiny. She couldn't have had that much to lose. "He's been in hell," she repeated.

Garrett took her hand into his. "Like Lucifer's hell?"

She took the bracelet back and gazed at it lovingly. "Yes. I could smell it on him."

"What does that mean?" Garrett asked. "While Charley and Reyes were fighting the Shade demons, he was sent back to hell?"

"Dragged," she said. "He was dragged back. After all, what does Satan do best?"

"Lie," Robert said.

She grinned weakly. "Okay, second best."

Robert lowered his head knowingly. "He takes advantage of every situation. While we were looking to the left, he stole in on the right and dragged that poor kid back to hell."

"He only looked like a kid," Garrett reminded him. "He is centuries old."

Robert sank into the chair beside Beep. "But he was a slave in hell, Swopes. An escaped one, prophesied to be by Elwyn's side during the uprising. To help bring Lucifer down. Lucy does not forgive easily."

Garrett hadn't forgotten. His son had been prophesized about in a very similar way. "What you're saying is, it probably wasn't a day at the spa for him."

"That kind of torture...it changes a man. Even a Daeva."

"How did you do it?" Beep asked Garrett for the seventeenth time.

He laughed softly. "I don't think I did. I think when Hayal died, the barrier came down of its own accord."

She shook her head. "Elemental light doesn't work like that."

He took her hand. "I don't know what to tell you, sweet pea. I mean, Osh got in. How did he do it?"

"That's number 1,248."

"Twelve forty-eight?"

"Yes. My list of questions for when I finally get to talk to Osh'ekiel."

"That's a lot of questions."

"You should see the list I have for my parents."

He laughed. All Garrett remembered was the spear protruding out of Beep's chest. The others told him how it'd happened. How he'd hit the barrier until it cracked and light streamed out of it like lightning. As though it short-circuited. They swore the lightning went through him, but he never felt it.

The doc finished going over Beep's chart, seemingly oblivious to their conversation, and gave Beep a quick once-over. "How are you doing, love?"

"Good. Can I go home now?"

Her face softened. "You are home, sweetheart."

"Oh, right."

"But you can have all the ice cream you want."

The transformation from pre-ice-cream comment to post-ice-cream comment was nothing short of miraculous. The mere mention of the creamy dessert seemed to breathe new life into her patient. "Really?"

"Doctor's orders."

"Did you hear that?" Beep asked both men. "You're my witnesses if Grandma asks."

Garret chuckled. "Okay, but if it comes to fisticuffs, I'm crying off."

* * * *

"Garrett, we can hardly get married when you're still in love with another woman." Two weeks later, Marika lay in Garrett's arms. The lovely ones with all the muscles and tattoos.

They were in his suite with Zaire asleep in what used to be Garrett's guest room. They'd moved in, but he kept insisting that they get married. So, she kept coming up with excuses why they couldn't. She'd just gotten her latest test results back.

Their situations were turning out startlingly similar to his growing up. Girl tricks man into getting her pregnant, then she dies and leaves child to face the world alone. Only Zaire would have Garrett, and he was a fantastic father.

"What the ever-loving fuck are you talking about?" he asked her. "I haven't dated another woman in years."

"Her," she said, trying to coax the sad truth out of him.

"Her?" he asked.

"Charley."

He choked on absolutely nothing and coughed for a solid minute.

"Charley? As in Davidson? Charles? As in the wife of Reyes Farrow, the son of Satan, the guy who is a god and is now some kind of celestial space matter floating around us and being all…not here? That Charley?"

"Precisely."

"And here I thought you were the stable one in this relationship. The sensible one."

"Garrett, you've been in love with her for years. You were in love with her when we met. I knew she would be my only obstacle, because the love, the romantic love, was unrequited."

"This is better than going to the movies."

"She loved you, Garrett. You need to know that. So, so much. I saw it every time she looked at you."

"With contempt and derision?"

"And you…well, you loved her, too. Deeply."

"Yes. Like I love my truck. Or my favorite sitcom."

"I just think—wait. You have a favorite sitcom?"

He crossed his arms over his chest. "I do."

"What is it?"

For some reason, it was important to her. So naturally, he refused to answer. "I'll tell you what," he said instead. "You guess, and if you guess it right, I get to kiss you wherever I want."

Excitement at the thought bubbled up like champagne fizzing inside her.

"Every time you guess wrong, you have to kiss me wherever I want."

"Absolutely not. You'll cheat."

"I would never."

"Please."

"Okay, I'll write it down, and you can keep it. But you can't look. That way, you'll know if I cheat."

"Yeah, after the fact."

"Fine. If I cheat, I'll cook you my famous low-carb cinnamon pancakes for breakfast."

"With bananas?"

"With bananas. Although that kind of screws up the low-carb genius of it all."

"Deal," she said before he changed his mind. She reached over him and grabbed a pen and paper from his nightstand.

"Don't look," he warned, so she turned her head. Reluctantly.

After a few seconds, he folded the paper and handed it to her. "Okay, guess away, but get ready for deep—oh so deep—exploration."

She wiggled in anticipation. "Well, it's probably something manly. Like *Full House* or *The Golden Girls*."

He laughed softly and made a circle in the air with his index finger, indicating he wanted her to turn over, so he could get at her backside, but he stopped mid-twirl and frowned over at her. "What did you say?"

"*Full House* or *The Golden Girls*."

"What the f—? Did you look at the paper?"

Her jaw fell to her chest. "Are you kidding me?" She tore open the note. "Your favorite sitcom is *The Golden Girls*?" She fairly screeched it; she was in such disbelief.

"You looked at the paper."

"I most certainly did not."

"Then you watched me write it, and you figured out what I wrote by the movement of the pen."

"Is that even a real thing?"

"Yes. And if not, how did you do that?"

She shrugged. "It's my favorite, too."

"Really?" he asked, seeming surprised.

A soft knock sounded on the bedroom door.

"Come in," Garrett said.

"No, wait," Marika squeaked, then ducked her head under the covers.

She peeked out in time to see Elwyn walk in carrying a breakfast tray. "Surprise!"

The girl's enthusiasm was contagious. And she looked amazing.

"I can't believe you've healed so quickly," Marika said as Elwyn put the tray on their nightstand. "You look like a different girl."

"It's the ice cream."

"You think?" Garrett asked, his grin just as infectious.

"I brought Marika orange juice."

"Oh, thank you." She sat up, careful to keep the covers at a decent level.

She watched as Elwyn took out a scalpel and cut a thin line across her wrist. Marika gasped as she put three drops of blood into Marika's glass then stirred it up with a spoon.

She handed it to her and said, "Drink."

Marika didn't take it. "Oh, gosh, I am stuffed. I couldn't fit another drop."

The girl, so wise beyond her years, smiled patiently. "I have always loved you."

"Elwyn, I've always loved you too."

"You gave me ice cream even though Grandma and Grandpa don't let me eat sugar."

"They don't let you eat sugar?" she asked, mortified.

"Not unless I'm mortally wounded. And you let me stay up watching scary movies. Grandma and Grandpa never let me watch scary movies, though they might now that I'm older."

"Oh, my God. They are never going to let me keep you again."

"And you listened to me. Really listened. You never treated me like…like *she-shu*."

"Well, I try not to treat anyone like *she-shu*. It's rude."

Elwyn laughed. "You always treated me as an equal."

She sat back and looked into her eyes. "That's where you're wrong, beautiful. I am nowhere near your equal."

"You think you are lower? You think you're *she-shu*?"

"Of course, I am. You are destined for such greatness. No one on this planet is your equal."

"You don't know?"

"Know what, love?"

Elwyn cleared her throat and handed her the glass. "Drink."

"If I do, will you make Zaire your special blueberry oatmeal for breakfast?"

She giggled. "Yes."

Marika glanced at Garrett, and she had the sneaking suspicion that he knew about her illness. Her pulse quickened as she lifted the glass to her lips, but she stopped and asked, "Elwyn, will this do what it did for the hellhounds? Will this…?" She couldn't say the words, and her hand began shaking.

"Yes," Elwyn said, pushing it to Marika's lips.

She squeezed her lids shut and downed it in two huge gulps. Then she put a hand to her mouth, a familiar sting in the backs of her eyes. Was this really happening? No months of chemo? Of nausea or fatigue or hair loss? No twelve percent?

Elwyn leaned in and whispered, "You are destined for great things, too."

Garrett took the glass and looked at Elwyn. "Now you just need to convince her to marry me."

"I've tried, but you're a hard sell. Maybe you should take up salsa dancing. You know, pad your resume."

He laughed softly and shook his head. "You vanished when you were five and have been away for almost a decade on some interdimensional walkabout. How do you even know what *pad your resume* means?"

"*The Golden Girls*."

"*The Golden Girls?*"

"Yes, *The Golden Girls*. Everything you need to know about life is on *The Golden Girls*, and you watched that show religiously. I couldn't help but pick up some pointers."

"Oh, yeah. That explains a lot."

Marika elbowed the man beside her. "Let me get this straight. You've recruited Elwyn to try and convince me to marry you?"

"You left me no choice."

She gave him her best deadpan, then said to Elwyn, "He doesn't want to marry me. He just feels guilty for making me cry the other night."

"He does, actually," she said. "When I touch someone like this"— she pushed her fingertips against his forehead—"I can tell if they are lying. He's definitely not lying."

"Wait, for real?" Garrett asked. "You can do that?"

"Yep. I know my mom could just kind of feel it, but I have to actually touch a person to know. I don't have to touch their forehead like this." She pressed again. "But it's funny."

"You're a riot," Garrett said.

"Okay, then." Marika grabbed her phone and started scrolling.

"What are you looking up?" Elwyn asked.

"The justice of the peace. We are doing this now before he changes his mind."

* * * *

Garrett looked at the sign again. There was a new coffee shop in town, and he just happened to know the proprietors. Nice couple. The wife was a tad unstable, the husband a bit volatile, but they worked well together.

He walked in. A bell overhead announced his arrival. The place sparkled with shiny newness, all dark woods and clean lines as he walked to the counter and looked at the woman he hadn't seen in over five years. She hadn't changed a bit. Same long, chestnut hair. Same gold eyes. Same smirk.

She gave him her best one, her smirks the stuff of legend, as she wiped down the counter. "Fancy meeting you here."

The smirk he offered her back was more sheepish than smartass.

"Sorry I lost your kid."

Her husband, the enigmatic Reyes Farrow, appeared in the pass-through window. "The fuck, Swopes?"

He cringed. "In my defense, I didn't know she could freaking teleport through the dead."

"Departed," Charley corrected a microsecond before she squealed and rushed around the counter to hug him.

"I can't believe you're back," he said into her hair, pulling her tight.

"Stop molesting my wife," Reyes said, his features just as striking as they had been when they ascended.

She stood back to look at him. "Our plan was to keep her safe from supernatural threats within the confines of Santa Fe County. To give her as normal an upbringing as possible. Clearly, that's not going to happen."

"She is something else, Charles."

Reyes came out of the kitchen and offered his hand.

"We tried to find her," Charley said. "We searched hundreds of worlds. Thousands of dimensions. It was like a needle in a haystack the size of Australia."

"She was in your hell at some point."

"Marmalade?" Charley squeaked in surprise.

Leave it to Charley Davidson to name a hell dimension after a jar of preserved fruit.

"Did she meet the gang?"

"Were the members of *the gang* named after frou-frou coffee beverages?"

She clasped her hands over her chest. "She did meet them. I hope they're okay."

"I think she favored Mocha Latte."

"Don't we all. Such a sweetheart."

"She can fight," he added.

"Mocha?"

"Your daughter."

"I guess that's a good thing."

"That she is not only her mother's daughter but her father's as well?"

"She'll need those skills when the time comes." Every time Charley talked about the pending war with Satan, sadness overtook her. Garrett knew she would do anything to protect her from that. Who the hell knew? The prophecies could be wrong. Even though, by that point, he'd found seven other texts corroborating his original findings. But still.

"Have you seen Osh since the battle?" Reyes asked.

"Not yet, but he's around. I'm certain of it."

"I can't believe he found her." Charley turned dreamy again. "He tracked her across a dozen planes."

"You know how to pick 'em," Garrett told her.

She beamed at him. "I sure do." She looked out the window and seemed to follow someone with her gaze. "She won't know us."

"Beep? How could she not know you? She's seen dozens of pictures."

"She won't recognize us," Reyes said. "We don't want to interfere with what you and the Loehrs are doing."

"That makes sense," Garrett said, his voice dripping with sarcasm. "She could use you guys, you know."

"Someday. For now…"

The door opened, and the bell chimed again. Garrett turned to see the little hellion walking in. Her face was full of awe as she took in the new shop.

Garrett jumped up and rushed to her. "Hey, Beep. How'd you get here?"

She pointed across the street. Garrett turned but only saw a woman standing there who made Cookie's clothing choices look positively planned.

"Oh, don't look right at her!" Beep took his arm and steered him toward the counter.

"Why?" he asked, suddenly panicked. "Is she dead?" He was still having a hard time discerning the dead from the living. At least from a distance.

"Departed. Yes."

"You used her as a portal to get into town? Isn't that kind of, I don't know, violative?"

"What? Public transportation."

"I guess that's one way to define it." He didn't even want to know who she jumped through at the compound. He dared a glance over his shoulder. "I think she's coming in."

"Crap. Don't look at her." She shoved him into a booth and sat across from him.

"Why shouldn't I look at her?"

"I should have mentioned this at some point over the last few years. Oh well. How do I put it?" She drummed her fingers as she thought. "Let's just say there are a couple of departed, like Mitzi there, who carry a torch."

"They can do that?" he asked, impressed. "I didn't know they could carry anything."

She rolled her eyes, bringing out her inner teen. "Not physically. Emotionally."

"I don't understand."

"They have a crush on you."

"On me?"

"Yes. Don't look. She just came in."

He leaned close. "I'm flattered. I think."

"That's not all," Elwyn said under her breath. "They formed a coalition. It's called GSN. Garrett Swopes Now."

"Strange name for a coalition."

"There are only a couple of members. Four at the most. Maybe five."

"And what does this coalition represent?"

"Well, you." She cupped a hand on the side of her mouth. "And getting you to them."

He blinked at her. For a very long time. Ignoring the dead woman standing right next to their booth. "What does that mean, exactly?"

Beep rolled her eyes again. So much like her mother, it startled him. "What do you think? It means they want you on their side of the world."

"Their side?"

"Dead, Garrett. They want you dead. As in your physical body passed so you can exist in the spiritual realm. Their realm. Stop looking at her."

"Can't she hear us?"

"It's hard to say. Some departed aren't quite as in tune with the physical world as others."

"Ah." He looked over at Charley and Reyes, who were gazing at their daughter as if she'd just gotten back from hanging the moon. He glared at them. They were going to blow their cover before it even began. "Hey, how did you know where to find me?"

She gaped at him. "Mitzi. Aren't you even listening? She follows you everywhere, and if she figures out that you can see her...*calaboom*."

"What does that even mean?"

"It was an expletive."

"Did you just cuss at me in Nepaui?"

After a long pause, she said, "No."

"Hmm. So, if she figures out I can see her?"

"It would not be good. She'll never leave you alone. On the bright side, she and the girls have tried to kill you a couple of times."

He leaned over the table. "They can do that?"

"No. Well, not in theory."

"In theory?" he asked, his voice sounding like a six-year-old girl's. When she only shrugged, he continued. "And how is that the bright side?"

"Because now you can see them."

"And?"

"You'll know if they try to kill you again."

"That is not comforting."

"What can I get you two?"

Beep looked up at the server. "Cookie!"

Garrett gaped at her. "What are you doing here?"

Cookie beamed at them. "I just thought I could use a second job."

"Since when?" Garrett frowned.

"Since some friends of mine opened a new coffee shop. Water?"

Cookie poured Beep a glass of water first, then Garrett, but when she lifted the pitcher, she knocked his glass over. Cold water rushed over the side.

"Oh, my goodness," Cookie said, dabbing at his crotch with a towel. "This happens to me so often."

His face heated despite himself. "You don't say."

Beep, who would normally be giggling about now, had grown quiet. He looked up from being molested to find her staring at something behind the counter. He turned and watched as Charles busied herself with wiping down the brand new never been used register and Reyes busied himself with cooking for absolutely no one.

"Whatcha looking at?" he asked his breakfast companion.

Cookie finished drying his crotch and hurried back to the kitchen, probably to hide.

Beep blinked and shook her head. "I think they're the owners."

"I bet they are. Do you know them?"

She thought and then shook her head. "I feel like I do, but I guess not. Nothing is coming to mind."

Wondering how the hell they'd managed to wipe Beep's memory of them with all the pictures she'd grown up with, he asked, "What do you feel like?"

"Sometimes, I feel like a nut."

"You watch too much TV. To eat."

"I feel like a mocha latte for starters."

"Good choice." He reached over his shoulder and scratched his back. It still itched from his run-in with Hayal.

Cookie came back, brandishing a T-shirt. "I brought a fresh shirt. I can throw yours in the dryer."

He chuckled and lifted it over his head. "This really isn't necessary, hon."

"If we had jeans, I'd dry those, too."

"I think you did a great job of that already."

Her cheeks blossomed the prettiest pink as he slipped on the tee. But Beep was staring at him now. Her eyes round.

"What's the matter, sweet pea?" he asked.

She blinked, pointed to his shoulder, the same one with scars still visible from the attack, and said quietly, "Did Hayal scratch you?"

He hadn't wanted her to worry. "He did, but I'm okay. Thanks to you." When she didn't say anything, he asked, "Is that bad?"

She scooted down in her seat and busied herself with her phone.

"Elwyn Alexandra Loehr, is that bad?"

It took her a good thirty seconds, but she finally shook her head. "No. Not at all. It's probably nothing."

"What's probably nothing?"

"Well, Nepaui scratches tend to…change people."

"Change people?"

"It still doesn't explain how you broke the light barrier, though. It's just not possible."

"What do you mean, change people?"

"Still, they got my blood into you really fast, right? You should be fine."

"Change people in what way?" he asked, growing more nervous by the second.

"It's not important."

"Elwyn," he warned.

She released a long sigh before answering. "Fine. You know those creatures we fought?"

"Yes."

"Let's just say they weren't originally Nepaui."

"Okay. What were they?"

"It's hard to say. They could have been any number of beings before fighting a Nepaui and getting scratched."

"Beep," he said from between clenched teeth. "Am I going to turn into one of those creatures?"

"Of course, not." She shook her head. "Probably not. I mean, they gave you my blood." She glanced at the ceiling to do the math. "I'd say you have, I don't know, one chance in ten."

"Of turning into one of those things?" His pulse quickened, and the edges of his vision grew dark.

"No, silly. Of *not* turning into one of those things."

He scraped a hand down his face. "Fuck."

* * * *

From 1001 Dark Nights and Darynda Jones, discover The Gravedigger's Son, coming May 11, 2021.

The Gravedigger's Son
A Charley Davidson Novella
By Darynda Jones
Coming May 11, 2021

The job should have been easy.

Get in. Assess the situation. Get out. But for veteran tracker Quentin Rutherford, things get sticky when the girl he's loved since puberty shows up, conducting her own investigation into the strange occurrences of the small, New Mexico town. He knew it would be a risk coming back to the area, but he had no idea Amber Kowalski had become a bona fide PI, investigating things that go bump in the night. He shouldn't be surprised, however. She can see through the dead as clearly as he can. The real question is, can she see through him?

But is anything that's worth it ever easy?

To say that Amber is shocked to see her childhood crush would be the understatement of her fragile second life. One look at him tells her everything she needs to know. He's changed. So drastically she barely recognizes him. He is savage now, a hardened—in all the right places—demon hunter, and she is simply the awkward, lovestruck girl he left behind.

But she doesn't have time to dwell on the past. A supernatural entity has set up shop, and it's up to them to stop it before it kills again.

While thousands of questions burn inside her, she has to put her concern over him, over what he's become, aside for now. Because he's about to learn one, undeniable fact: she's changed, too.

Sign up for the 1001 Dark Nights Newsletter
and be entered to win a Tiffany Key necklace.

There's a contest every month!

Go to www.1001DarkNights.com to subscribe.

**As a bonus, all subscribers can download
FIVE FREE exclusive books!**

Discover 1001 Dark Nights Collection Seven

Visit www.1001DarkNights.com for more information.

THE BISHOP by Skye Warren
A Tanglewood Novella

TAKEN WITH YOU by Carrie Ann Ryan
A Fractured Connections Novella

DRAGON LOST by Donna Grant
A Dark Kings Novella

SEXY LOVE by Carly Phillips
A Sexy Series Novella

PROVOKE by Rachel Van Dyken
A Seaside Pictures Novella

RAFE by Sawyer Bennett
An Arizona Vengeance Novella

THE NAUGHTY PRINCESS by Claire Contreras
A Sexy Royals Novella

THE GRAVEYARD SHIFT by Darynda Jones
A Charley Davidson Novella

CHARMED by Lexi Blake
A Masters and Mercenaries Novella

SACRIFICE OF DARKNESS by Alexandra Ivy
A Guardians of Eternity Novella

THE QUEEN by Jen Armentrout
A Wicked Novella

BEGIN AGAIN by Jennifer Probst
A Stay Novella

VIXEN by Rebecca Zanetti
A Dark Protectors/Rebels Novella

SLASH by Laurelin Paige
A Slay Series Novella

THE DEAD HEAT OF SUMMER by Heather Graham
A Krewe of Hunters Novella

WILD FIRE by Kristen Ashley
A Chaos Novella

MORE THAN PROTECT YOU by Shayla Black
A More Than Words Novella

LOVE SONG by Kylie Scott
A Stage Dive Novella

CHERISH ME by J. Kenner
A Stark Ever After Novella

SHINE WITH ME by Kristen Proby
A With Me in Seattle Novella

And new from Blue Box Press:

TEASE ME by J. Kenner
A Stark International Novel

FROM BLOOD AND ASH by Jennifer L. Armentrout
A Blood and Ash Novel

QUEEN MOVE by Kennedy Ryan

THE BUTTERFLY ROOM by Lucinda Riley

Betwixt

A Paranormal Women's Fiction Novel
By Darynda Jones
Now Available!

A Paranormal Women's Fiction with a bit of class, and a lot of sass, for anyone who feels like age is just a number!

Divorced, desperate, and destitute, former restaurateur Defiance Dayne finds out she has been bequeathed a house by a complete stranger. She is surprised, to say the least, and her curiosity gets the better of her. She leaves her beloved Phoenix and heads to one of the most infamous towns in America: Salem, Massachusetts.

She's only there to find out why a woman she's never met would leave her a house. A veritable castle that has seen better days. She couldn't possibly accept it, but the lawyer assigned to the case practically begs her to take it off her hands, mostly because she's scared of it. The house. The inanimate structure that, as far as Dephne can tell, has never hurt a fly.

Though it does come with some baggage. A pesky neighbor who wants her gone. A scruffy cat who's a bit of a jerk. And a handyman bathed in ink who could moonlight as a supermodel for GQ.

She decides to give it three days, and not because of the model. She feels at home in Salem. Safe. But even that comes to a screeching halt when people begin knocking on her door day and night, begging for her help to locate their lost objects.

Come to find out, they think she's a witch. And after a few mysterious mishaps, Dephne is beginning to wonder if they're right.

* * * *

I glanced at the zippered bag the real estate agent handed me somewhere between the tornado and her nickel-slick getaway, wondering once again if I'd just made the biggest mistake of my life.

She'd had no answers for me over the phone and apparently that hadn't changed.

"I don't understand," I'd told her when she called three days ago. "Someone left me a house?"

"Yes. Free and clear. It's all yours. Mrs. Goode left explicit instructions in her will and I promised her—"

"I'm sorry. I don't know a Ruthie Goode. There must be a mistake."

"She said you'd say that."

"Mrs. Richter, people don't just leave strangers houses."

"She said you'd say that, too."

"Not to mention the fact that I live in Arizona. I've never even been to Massachusetts."

"And that. I don't know what to tell you, sweetheart. Mrs. Goode left very detailed instructions. You must accept the house in person within the next seventy-two hours to take possession. Either way, it cannot be sold to anyone else for a year. If you don't take it, it'll just sit there, abandoned and vulnerable."

Abandoned and vulnerable. No words in the English language made me more uncomfortable.

Three days.

Well, maybe syphilis.

I had three days to decide.

And moist.

I turned to the abode known as Percival, took another good look at what a woman I'd never met named Ruthie Goode left me, then climbed back into the bug and pulled her into Percival's driveway.

My life had been punctuated by the strange and unexplained. I was flypaper for what others called the weird. Countless friends and coworkers had remarked on the fact that if there was an unstable sentient being within a ten-mile radius, it would find its way to me eventually. Dog. Cat. Woman. Man. Iguana.

I once had to track down the parents of a toddler who thought I was her dead aunt Lucille. An aunt she'd never met, according to the aforementioned procreators.

Everyone called these admirers, for lack of a better term, weird. I called them charming. Quirky. Eccentric.

This, however, took the raspberry covered chocolate cheesecake. I'd only been bequeathed one other item from a departed member of society, and that was when Greg Sanchez handed me his half-eaten ice cream cone seconds before falling into a volcano.

That field trip did not end well.

I grabbed my overnight bag and paused again to get a better look at Percival.

He was already growing on me, damn him. I had a thing for the broody ones. The dark ones with deep, invisible scars who looked like they'd fought a thousand battles. Percival definitely fit the bill.

Filling my lungs with crisp New England air, air that held the smoky scent of wood burning from hearths nearby, I stepped to Percy's front door, took the key out of the zippered bag Mrs. Richter had given me, and entered.

I stopped just inside the foyer so Percy and I could chat. "Okay, Percy," I said aloud, only feeling a little silly. "Do you mind if I call you Percy?" I let my eyes adjust to the dimness inside the house. "Looks like it's just you and me."

About Darynda Jones

NY Times and *USA Today* Bestselling Author Darynda Jones has won numerous awards for her work, including a prestigious RITA, a Golden Heart, and a Daphne du Maurier, and her books have been translated into 18 languages. As a born storyteller, Darynda grew up spinning tales of dashing damsels and heroes in distress for any unfortunate soul who happened by, and she is ever so grateful for the opportunity to carry on that legacy. She currently has two series with St. Martin's Press: The Charley Davidson Series and the Darklight Trilogy. She lives in the Land of Enchantment, also known as New Mexico, with her husband and two beautiful sons, the Mighty, Mighty Jones Boys.

She can be found at http://www.daryndajones.com

Discover 1001 Dark Nights

Visit www.1001DarkNights.com for more information.

COLLECTION ONE
FOREVER WICKED by Shayla Black
CRIMSON TWILIGHT by Heather Graham
CAPTURED IN SURRENDER by Liliana Hart
SILENT BITE: A SCANGUARDS WEDDING by Tina Folsom
DUNGEON GAMES by Lexi Blake
AZAGOTH by Larissa Ione
NEED YOU NOW by Lisa Renee Jones
SHOW ME, BABY by Cherise Sinclair
ROPED IN by Lorelei James
TEMPTED BY MIDNIGHT by Lara Adrian
THE FLAME by Christopher Rice
CARESS OF DARKNESS by Julie Kenner

COLLECTION TWO
WICKED WOLF by Carrie Ann Ryan
WHEN IRISH EYES ARE HAUNTING by Heather Graham
EASY WITH YOU by Kristen Proby
MASTER OF FREEDOM by Cherise Sinclair
CARESS OF PLEASURE by Julie Kenner
ADORED by Lexi Blake
HADES by Larissa Ione
RAVAGED by Elisabeth Naughton
DREAM OF YOU by Jennifer L. Armentrout
STRIPPED DOWN by Lorelei James
RAGE/KILLIAN by Alexandra Ivy/Laura Wright
DRAGON KING by Donna Grant
PURE WICKED by Shayla Black
HARD AS STEEL by Laura Kaye
STROKE OF MIDNIGHT by Lara Adrian
ALL HALLOWS EVE by Heather Graham
KISS THE FLAME by Christopher Rice
DARING HER LOVE by Melissa Foster
TEASED by Rebecca Zanetti
THE PROMISE OF SURRENDER by Liliana Hart

COLLECTION THREE
HIDDEN INK by Carrie Ann Ryan
BLOOD ON THE BAYOU by Heather Graham
SEARCHING FOR MINE by Jennifer Probst
DANCE OF DESIRE by Christopher Rice
ROUGH RHYTHM by Tessa Bailey
DEVOTED by Lexi Blake
Z by Larissa Ione
FALLING UNDER YOU by Laurelin Paige
EASY FOR KEEPS by Kristen Proby
UNCHAINED by Elisabeth Naughton
HARD TO SERVE by Laura Kaye
DRAGON FEVER by Donna Grant
KAYDEN/SIMON by Alexandra Ivy/Laura Wright
STRUNG UP by Lorelei James
MIDNIGHT UNTAMED by Lara Adrian
TRICKED by Rebecca Zanetti
DIRTY WICKED by Shayla Black
THE ONLY ONE by Lauren Blakely
SWEET SURRENDER by Liliana Hart

COLLECTION FOUR
ROCK CHICK REAWAKENING by Kristen Ashley
ADORING INK by Carrie Ann Ryan
SWEET RIVALRY by K. Bromberg
SHADE'S LADY by Joanna Wylde
RAZR by Larissa Ione
ARRANGED by Lexi Blake
TANGLED by Rebecca Zanetti
HOLD ME by J. Kenner
SOMEHOW, SOME WAY by Jennifer Probst
TOO CLOSE TO CALL by Tessa Bailey
HUNTED by Elisabeth Naughton
EYES ON YOU by Laura Kaye
BLADE by Alexandra Ivy/Laura Wright
DRAGON BURN by Donna Grant
TRIPPED OUT by Lorelei James

STUD FINDER by Lauren Blakely
MIDNIGHT UNLEASHED by Lara Adrian
HALLOW BE THE HAUNT by Heather Graham
DIRTY FILTHY FIX by Laurelin Paige
THE BED MATE by Kendall Ryan
NIGHT GAMES by CD Reiss
NO RESERVATIONS by Kristen Proby
DAWN OF SURRENDER by Liliana Hart

COLLECTION FIVE
BLAZE ERUPTING by Rebecca Zanetti
ROUGH RIDE by Kristen Ashley
HAWKYN by Larissa Ione
RIDE DIRTY by Laura Kaye
ROME'S CHANCE by Joanna Wylde
THE MARRIAGE ARRANGEMENT by Jennifer Probst
SURRENDER by Elisabeth Naughton
INKED NIGHTS by Carrie Ann Ryan
ENVY by Rachel Van Dyken
PROTECTED by Lexi Blake
THE PRINCE by Jennifer L. Armentrout
PLEASE ME by J. Kenner
WOUND TIGHT by Lorelei James
STRONG by Kylie Scott
DRAGON NIGHT by Donna Grant
TEMPTING BROOKE by Kristen Proby
HAUNTED BE THE HOLIDAYS by Heather Graham
CONTROL by K. Bromberg
HUNKY HEARTBREAKER by Kendall Ryan
THE DARKEST CAPTIVE by Gena Showalter

COLLECTION SIX
DRAGON CLAIMED by Donna Grant
ASHES TO INK by Carrie Ann Ryan
ENSNARED by Elisabeth Naughton
EVERMORE by Corinne Michaels
VENGEANCE by Rebecca Zanetti
ELI'S TRIUMPH by Joanna Wylde

CIPHER by Larissa Ione
RESCUING MACIE by Susan Stoker
ENCHANTED by Lexi Blake
TAKE THE BRIDE by Carly Phillips
INDULGE ME by J. Kenner
THE KING by Jennifer L. Armentrout
QUIET MAN by Kristen Ashley
ABANDON by Rachel Van Dyken
THE OPEN DOOR by Laurelin Paige
CLOSER by Kylie Scott
SOMETHING JUST LIKE THIS by Jennifer Probst
BLOOD NIGHT by Heather Graham
TWIST OF FATE by Jill Shalvis
MORE THAN PLEASURE YOU by Shayla Black
WONDER WITH ME by Kristen Proby
THE DARKEST ASSASSIN by Gena Showalter

Discover Blue Box Press

TAME ME by J. Kenner
TEMPT ME by J. Kenner
DAMIEN by J. Kenner
TEASE ME by J. Kenner
REAPER by Larissa Ione
THE SURRENDER GATE by Christopher Rice
SERVICING THE TARGET by Cherise Sinclair

On Behalf of 1001 Dark Nights,

Liz Berry, M.J. Rose, and Jillian Stein would like to thank ~

Steve Berry
Doug Scofield
Benjamin Stein
Kim Guidroz
Social Butterfly PR
Asha Hossain
Chris Graham
Chelle Olson
Kasi Alexander
Jessica Johns
Dylan Stockton
Richard Blake
and Simon Lipskar

Made in the USA
San Bernardino, CA
19 June 2020